To
Yvonne —
with love & best wishes

Hasan Robin

Books by the same author

The Fatal Flaw (1987) Published by Arthur H. Stockwell Ltd. Devon, U.K.

Journey to Life (2015) Published by, Wesbrook Bay Books, Vancouver BC Canada.

The Medallion (2017) Published by, AuthorHouse, Bloomington, IN, USA.

The Rescue, (2017) Published by, AuthorHouse, Bloomington, IN, USA.

WAKING MARS

H. P. KABIR

authorHOUSE®

AuthorHouse™
1663 Liberty Drive
Bloomington, IN 47403
www.authorhouse.com
Phone: 1 (800) 839-8640

Published by AuthorHouse   06/11/2018

ISBN: 978-1-5462-4491-2 (sc)
ISBN: 978-1-5462-4489-9 (hc)
ISBN: 978-1-5462-4490-5 (e)

Library of Congress Control Number: 2018906480

Print information available on the last page.

CONTENTS

Dedicated to:

My mother Aeysha & my father Shah Jehan
My mother-in-law, Arfah and father-in - law, Dr. A.A. Khan
My brothers Behram & Reda
&
My wife Rasheda. Daughters: Shahnaz and Tanya,
Their husbands Tahir and Paul,
Grandchildren: Zaid and Emad
&
My sister Latifa. Her husband Salim and children,
Saira, Shazia and Anwar and his wife, Rebecca,
&
Grandchildren: Lara, Adam, Zachary and Leila

PROLOGUE

Waking Mars is the third in the series about the aliens who accidently found Earth and lived on it for millenniums until recently, starting with '*The Medallion*' in which an artifact was found, got them involved with four locals who became trusted friends. It led to an adventure finding a device and when found, the message it contained was read, the world termed it as a hoax. Disappointed with the reception it received, the aliens decided to leave Earth.

In the sequel, '*The Rescue*', comfortably settled on their world Urna, the aliens spotted and destroyed an asteroid heading towards Earth which could have annihilated all life. They returned to inform them of their goodwill to save humanity from extinction, but found an old alien adversary who had taken control of the planet. After getting rid of them, they felt obliged to help in setting up a New World Order to govern, supervise and maintain peace and harmony from the pandemonium of different causes that had plagued the world. There were oppositions but had to be entrenched by an offer no one could refuse.

In *Waking Mars,* after returning to their planet, the aliens continued the work they had started years ago to rejuvenate the Martian atmosphere and help a lifeform to get rid of creatures which threatened their lives. Meanwhile, on Earth the building of the New World Order was shattered by a bomb killing all in attendance by a clandestine organisation which proclaimed itself as the new authority, the aliens once again returned to the rescue.

Out of nowhere suddenly an alien spaceship was spotted, when encountered, to their surprise the occupants were descendants of former residents of Earth who had left due to a natural disaster, thousands of years ago. With their help, the revitalisation of Mars was enhanced. Domed cities were built, a few were to host selected immigrants from Earth. The acclimatisation of Mars was a success. However, during the festivity an alarming news came in about an enigmatic force threatening life and infrastructure on Earth.

CHAPTER 1

It had been twelve years since the aliens had setup the New World Order on Earth leaving the Guardian in charge. The humans who had chosen to leave with them since their first encounter twenty three years earlier involving a medallion and the search for a device found in a pyramid placed by the aliens, millenniums earlier were well settled on Urna, the aliens' world, sandwiched between Jupiter and Saturn. Each one of them had a task. (i) David, Jim and Saeed ran the library and the museum. Daniel and his wife Fiona managed a special school of scholars and persons with extrasensory perception abilities, Sam and his Jinn wife Aishtra assisted Ayond, the alien lady running the affairs of the planet. Jim's wife busied herself teaching cooking, embroidery and gossip. The group made a happy family and they were trusted.

Ashtok, their Supreme High, was a highly sophisticated intelligent android, more humanoid than an artificial intelligent machine on whom the aliens depended upon its wisdom and extra-ordinary abilities. Only some years ago it was transformed into a living form from a stationery cubic by the Guardian who too was an android. (ii) Their features were human, the only differences were their bodily metallic shine and the height, bit taller than the average human.

1

It was one splendid afternoons on Urna, sitting on the open terrace under an extended branch of a large tree Ayond looked up and said in a tuneful tone, "I love you, it was not long that I planted you." She turned and looked at Ashtok, "You think I am crazy talking to my tree, it has been my companion friend in my lonely moments and I am sure it understands me that's why it has grown its branches right over my terrace, giving me shade from the scorching artificial emissions of the reflected sun's rays. Tell me Ashtok, are you really happy with your new name. To me and the people of our planet Urna you will always be the Supreme High. It made no difference from when you were a stationery cube or what you are now, a *living entity,* capable of walking around like all of us. Thanks to the Guardian who made it possible. Why did you chose *Ashtok* as a name?"

"As you know in our language it means *'one of you'* and it is most appropriate for me rising from that state to be a living being just like any other person. So the name explains it all."

"All those years you were a thinking brain encased in a metallic cube sitting endlessly in one spot. Must have been boring."

"On the contrary when you are made in a certain form you accept it as the putative thing, no desire for anything except the functions you are supposed to do. When the Guardian came with the idea just a few years ago and discussed it with me, I was hesitant at first, his team of engineers convinced me and asked me what kind of shape I preferred, feminine or masculine. I chose the latter. They designed my looks similar to the Guardian with a gilded shine and a bit taller. Also incorporated the functions to transform into light waves or photons and to travel at high speed like him. Just to reflect, on the planet where I came from, I was in my former form, a stationary cube and was referred to as the super machine and along with the people who had made me, we had created the Keepers, one of them landed on your planet and you named him the Guardian. They were made to help in running the daily routine affairs of the planet since the population of living beings was declining due to an enigmatic rainfall with a green tinge, which caused sterility to all lifeforms and to some extent plants. Those people had reached the zenith of creation mentally and physically. When they gradually died out, only us the machines were left, so I decided and sent the Keepers to go and seek new worlds where they could be useful. Before leaving they housed me in a secure place until such time one of them may return and take me to a new home. Because of the Guardian I came to be in your world, Urna, much before it was jettisoned out by its binary system. That was also many years before your time Ayond." (iii)

Ayond reflected on the people who made him, "They must have been very special."

"They were indeed, made of flesh and blood and understood the meaning of life. I shall always remember them with respect, after all they were my makers."

Their conversation drifted to the time when Urna was jettisoned out of its orbit as a result of a tug of war between its two suns, a binary system with seven planets.

"From what I read, it was you who had the capability to control the planet's magnetic field and its drift into the void of space as a rouge planet. Less than one third of the populace miraculously survived the ordeal. By chance Urna entered this solar system and on your advice the Guardian evacuated as many as possible to land on Earth as you were unsure of the planet's predicament, to be drawn towards the sun and swallowed or continue to drift indefinitely in space. Miraculously Urna survived, it was caught by the sun and placed into orbit between Jupiter and Saturn. You, the Guardian and none of the scientist were aware of our world's phenomenal survival until much later. However, it was a wise decision to instruct the Guardian to load spaceships with as many as they could carry to land them to safety. They landed on the rich fertile plains of five rivers, what is today the Indus Valley in Pakistan, that was some 15,000 years ago.

"Subsequently, later moved to the confluence of Euphrates and Tigress Rivers and the Nile Basin, did a commendable job in improving the living standards of the populace and thought them the art of cultivation. It was another wise decision to finally move to the British Isles. That was all before my time, I was born much later on Earth, like the present generation who moved back to Urna." Ayond recalled.

"Ayond, you love to recap the good old golden days of our stay on Earth, it was unfortunate we had to leave because of the arrogance of the people to whom we had contributed so much in improving their knowledge and welfare. Though we arrived there before the time of the rise of the first civilization, had an equal right to live on that world as the humans had. (iv). Furthermore not forgetting our return ten years later after the dramatic rescue of the human race from extinction by an asteroid the size of Deimos, and the removal of the reptilian aliens known as Xanthumians who literally dominated the planet and robbed it of its gold resources. In good fate we introduced The New World Order twelve years ago to bring about peace and tranquillity, had its ups and downs but we were satisfied with its progress. (v) We are now back on

Urna and progressing well with my project to wake up Mars which I had started many years ago."

Ayond was engrossed in the conversation, suddenly she burst loudly, "Forget about Earth and Mars for now, you have come today to enjoy my tea harvest and you have not yet taken one whiff. I have finished two cups and you have not looked at what is in front of you."

In front of him lay two saucers, in one, green fresh stems and the other with some tea leaves. Ashtok picked a stem and brought it to his nose. Moved it to and fro, took a deep inhale, waited a few second, then another. "Ummm," he hummed appreciatively. Picked a few leaves and put them in his mouth. Began to masticate, showing gratifying gestures, he removed the chewed remains and with a feeling of satisfaction he said sullenly, "If only I could have the real thing as in cups I would give you the world. You know I am a machine can't drink or eat, what a gift is to be a real living being of flesh and blood. Both have advantages and disadvantages." He paused and added, "How about calling your Earth friends, I love their company and they can enjoy some of your brew."

Ayond called David to collect all.

Soon they joined in and the conversation continued, "It has been sometime since we had the pleasure to sip the good old beverage," David said putting his cup down.

Ashtok said philosophically, "There are many good thing on Earth and one of them is you all. It was a wise decision to come to our world and you have made a good team working with us in various fields. It all began with Sam finding the medallion which started it all."(vi). He looked at him and said, "Sam, how is life

5

being married to a Jinn? Has she shown you some of her special abilities?"

Sam in an embarrassing tone, "Some, and they are most satisfying."

There was loud laughter and someone shouted, "How about explaining some of them."

"He will tell you privately, we don't want to embarrass him right now." Ashtok put in looking at Sam.

Sam was married to Aishtra, a Jinn, a specie with extraordinary abilities believe to exist on Earth. As a child she was rescued and brought up by Ayond when her parents had died in an air crash, she is now one of her assistants.

"How about you Jim are you happy?" Ashtok asked.

"Very happy, love my work. My wife is doubly happy with her women companions, teaching them our earthly popular dishes, such as barbeques, pizzas and some oriental cuisines, and they love it."

"Daniel how are you and Fiona fairing with imparting your noble ideas and learning ours."

"Ashtok, it could not be better, I am learning more than I can deliver."

"David you too have settled well keeping busy with our archives and museum affairs. And you Saeed, my Egyptian Pharaoh, you don't mind calling you that, after all you come from that land. We can't forget your valuable efforts to retrieve the device found in a pyramid. You are all contributing to the welfare of our community on Urna, and soon will include you to be part of a very special project which I have been working on for a long time. Shortly, I will tell you what it is.

"Imagine not long ago you were talking to me as a piece of metal, an intelligent one of course, sitting in a corner in Ayond's office, most of the time all by myself just waiting for company or requesting you to come and meet me. Now I am a living being. Thanks to the Guardian. He is doing well on Earth as head of the New World Order though he tells me there have been many defaulters to the rules and regulations. Many measures were imposed to correct the situations and in two extreme cases force had to be used." Ashtok said.

Ayond made a remark, "Had it been a human in his place, the whole exercise would have been a failure, too weak to handle delicate situations and would have lost control over the five permanent members and the nine executives that run the New World Order. It has been twelve years since we promulgated that form of governess. The ninety percent who are members are thriving beautifully, the remaining stubbornly refused to be part of this fraternity and are trouble makers, their multifarious activities are so subtle that we cannot pin point any wrong doing to reprimand them. If or when they surface, we will be waiting for them."

Ashtok added complacently, "In due course all will join in, when they begin to feel the pinch of being excluded from all international transactions and are reduced to a failed state. They will come begging to join the world community. Remember the old saying, 'Rome was not built in a day." He paused and looked at Ayond, "Can I have some more of those tea leaves before getting into my next subject." While he waited for an attendant to oblige, Ashtok said as if throwing a challenge. "On my next trip to Earth will visit tea gardens and collect the best shrubs to build my own nursery. In all our meetings or get to gathers, I will be served with a plate of shoots harvested by me," he stopped and looked at the others, "While you all can have your other concoctions."

The tea leaves were served and after relishing them Ashtok began. "I mentioned earlier about my special project. For a long time I had been working on vitalising or bringing Mars to life, the Guardian provided the data and our scientists did the field work. Ayond came in much later. Since I have become mobile we have achieved many strides. Our progress is remarkable, we are already getting positive indications of our accomplishments. I sometime sit and dream of what it would look like with people and children playing making a racket. Not forgetting Aishtra's people, the Jinn and perhaps many others.

"Initially very few humans will be selected, from Canada, a happy nation full of smiles and laughter and from the United States, the symbol of democracy who out of nothing have become the greatest power where dreams become reality. Selections from other parts of the world will be carried out after a thorough investigation by experts. Rich or poor will be treated alike.

"Imagine what life would be like on Mars, of course we will not give up Urna, it has turned out to be unique in every way, keeping in mind its location, sandwiched between the mighty Jupiter and glamourous Saturn. The scene from our world is breath taking. Developing Mars is an insurance, just in case we have to abandon Urna and perhaps a refuge for humans who want a better life. Our work on Mars had begun long time ago. We selected an area somewhere close to the South Pole where there is plenty of water trapped beneath the surface. An ocean like reservoir, with filtration the water is as good as any and would last for a thousand years. There are some more reservoirs elsewhere on the planet. They too should last for a long time before they are exhausted, hopefully before that, natural rain will compensate. Domed cities will be built on all locations where water is available. It is an ambitious task but workable. I am just counting the days when all this would come to fruition. You would then be citizens of three worlds, Urna, Mars and Earth."

Ayond was listening attentively and put a word of caution, "Of course we have to be careful not let Earth see our activities. Twice they almost stumbled on that area and we had to discretely eliminate the unmanned probes. Had we not, they would have surely discovered our most treasured secret which only a limited number of people on Urna know of. Another fear is, they would be sending astronauts to investigate the fate of their first Mars-1 mission five years ago, with a crew of three, two died in a freak accident and the third just vanished, though not in the real sense."

"Excuse me Ayond," David interrupted, "You just said, 'most treasured secret', what is it? And what did you mean by 'the third vanished, though not in the real sense'? What has happened to him?" David asked.

Before Ayond could reply, Ashtok interrupted, "For the time being it is a bit premature to talk about, but soon you will come to know. However, to change the subject, the Guardian had informed me, the Earth Space Agency is preparing to launch another mission to Mars to reach sometime in December 2042 with four astronauts, two male and two females. We don't want them to see what we are doing. It will depend where they land. Perhaps where their Mars – 1 landed five years ago to investigate the failure of that mission, collect some soil samples and depart. We will keep a strict vigilance, at any cost they must not see any of our activities. Finally let me tell you that by early next year my specially designed spaceship will be ready. Its configuration and the tricks it can perform are unimaginable, the best ever built by our engineers. You all will be the first to experience the luxuries within, when we go on its inaugural flight. Now if you excuse me, I have to leave, it has been a very stimulating afternoon. Thank you all for coming and to Ayond for being a generous host, must have more of it often.

"Your request is my command," Ayond said with a theatrical bow.

CHAPTER 2

It was just before Christmas on Earth in the year 2042, a better equipped spaceship, Mars-2 arrived and orbited Mars with four astronauts, two males and two females. Their mission was to find out what had happened to the only survivor of the Mars–1 three men crew, who had vanished without a trace after the death of the other two, five years ago. His last message to Earth Space Agency was that he was going to explore a cave in which he found a written message addressed to him. He had no explanation by whom it was put there. His fellow companions had died before he had discovered the cave.

Ashtok had sent a crew in an invisible vessel perched on Phobos, one of the Martian moons to watch the astronaut's activities.

The Mars – 2 astronauts got into a shuttle and landed at the site near the Habitat, the name given to the living quarters where the Mars-1 crew had stayed.

Not far from the entrance to the Habitat they stopped at two well marked graves with names of the astronauts who had died, they paused for a moment in prayer then proceeded.

Inside, the lights came on automatically, the air conditioning and ventilation system began to function as soon as the air lock shut behind them. The entire Habitat was spick and span as just been serviced. They searched the entire facility and did not find any belongings of the missing astronaut or of the deceased companions.

"He must have collected everything and taken them with him to wherever he has gone." One of the astronauts said.

"He must have known he would not be coming back, cleaned up the place and left. On the other hand, had he been in a fatal accident, all their belongings would have been here." Another said.

"But where could he have gone?" Annie exclaimed.

"Perhaps kidnapped by a Martian lady and is living happily ever after." Paula, the other female astronaut added with a giggle.

After an exhausting search, under a sleeping mattress a book was found, scribbled boldly on its cover, *"My diary".*

They all gathered and Jim, the captain began to read, "Page one says, October 9, 2037, I am alone now, for days just sit, eat and sleep. It is so boring, tried to leave but for some reason the ignition and the controls of the shuttle are jammed, it is as good as dead, with my limited rations, once consumed will die alone.

"Dear diary, it is another day, could not sleep for a long time, twisted and turned in bed. Woke up late, had breakfast, while having my coffee a thought struck me, why not go out and explore, spend my remaining days usefully instead of sitting gloomily bored and dejected. I will visit the location where my colleagues met their fate. More when I get back.

'I returned before sunset, what a day it was. No sooner when I reached there this morning, a freak wind began to blow hard. Looked around to find shelter, luckily not far from where I stood I saw an opening at the base of a towering mountain wall that stretched endlessly above me.'

"I hope he found shelter," someone interrupted.

"Why don't you just listen," the reader said hotly and began to read. "To my luck it was a cave, the wind was strong, bent double and battled my way in and coiled in a corner. It was a long wait before the wind subsided, I surveyed my surroundings, something was unnatural about that cave the walls were too smooth. The depth of the cave was only about twenty feet. With my gloved hand I fanned the surface and with my fingers tried to scrape some of its grit, it was hard and slippery. Tried with a pick axe, it just bounced back without leaving a mark. 'That is not a natural rock, how is it possible, who could have built it.' I said to myself as if addressing someone. With that enigma I decided to return early the next day to have sufficient time to explore. Can't sleep, keep thinking about the wall, what could have caused its surface to be solid and smooth. No natural causes could have made it, lava flow out of the question. Now going to bed.

"Dear diary, October 11. I have just returned back, what a day it was. No one would ever believe what had happened, I would have been in doubt had it not been for what is in front of me. Let me start from the time I left this morning. Parked my vehicle a short distance away from the cave, fully armed with some chemicals, a controlled explosive device, a shovel, pick axe and a bag to collect the gravel for sampling. As I entered a horrific sign greeted me, a cloth strip hung about a few feet from the ground on it said in

English, "Welcome Earth Man." I almost fainted, but screwed up my courage and cautiously threaded in. 'Some joker, but who, my two colleagues are dead, I buried them myself,' I said, talking to myself. Then a shiver ran up my spine and shouted, 'This is no joke, some thing or some creature is watching me,' impulsively I struck the sign with my pick axe and pulled it down. I hurried back to the Habitat. It is now spread on the floor as I am making this entry in my diary, keep glancing at it.

"Dear diary, I am confused. My dead colleagues may have been in that cave and as a practical joke had put up that sign, unfortunately as they left were blown by a freak gust of wind that smashed them against the mountain wall. But, if they had put this sign, why did I not see it yesterday, could not have missed it, or did I? No other possible explanation, definitely put by them, there is no other living soul on this dead world. I am going out right away and bury it next to them.

"I am back, buried it, put a heavy rock on top of it and marked it with a splash of white paint.'

One of the astronauts curiously interrupted, "How about checking it out."

They put on their space suits and went out. There was a rock between the two graves with faded white paint.

"Let us leave it for the night, dig it out in the morning." The captain suggested.

Before resuming to read, coffee was served, the rest sat and waited attentively facing the reader like a mother telling a fairy tale to her children.

"Where was I?" Jim murmured and began, "Last night I kept awake thinking of the possibility of intelligent life existing on Mars. But where are they, no structures or signs anywhere. Come what may, tomorrow I am going to that cave and perhaps there will be another message or may meet a Martian. A wild thought, what if he or she is a cannibal, I don't care to be barbequed or made a soup out of me. Sooner or later I am going to die on this planet, might as well get it done in a generous way." Jim stopped and finished his coffee.

"Jim hurry up and read on," Paula, one of the astronauts excitedly interjected.

"Will do my lady, but first can you please pick up those empty cups and take them away," Jim said in a comic tone and hand gestured theatrically pointing to the cups.

"Surely his two deceased colleagues had put that sign to play a joke on Joshua before they met their fate." Paula said, picking the cups and walked to the pantry.

"Soon we'll find out, I will read a little more and continue tomorrow, must get a good night's rest," Jim put in and began to read.

"I, Joshua Hindan have given up my desire to live as I have nothing in my world to go back to, no parents, family or anyone to care for me, at least I am one up on the whole human race, I have conquered space and now living on another world called Mars. I have no regrets. To you my diary, I say good night and if I am still alive tomorrow will fill in more pages.' With that Jim gently folded the pages and placed a pen as a page marker.

15

It was the second day of their arrival, the four astronauts eagerly went out to the spot where the reclining stone lay. Removed it and retrieved a bag, in it a six inch wide long strip of cloth like paper, they spread it on the ground holding both ends with their feet and read its contents. They exchanged glances.

"He was right, who else could have written this, and in English other than his fellow astronauts?" Jim said. On examining the quality of the cloth, he added, "This is not cloth, some kind of a fabric. A cloth would have withered or shown some decolouration after so many years. Can't guess what it is, I will do some tests on it. But we are left with the big question, who had written it?"

"As I said before, perhaps some Martians found Joshua, and took him away." Paula said.

Alex, one of the astronauts said with a bit of humour. "You may be right Paula, Joshua must have been kidnapped by a Martian lady and is happily settled, while we sweat looking for him."

Jim was not amused, "No time for jokes, let us get to work for what we have come. Alex, let us get into the shuttle and try to find that cave. Joshua mentioned it being at the bottom of a wall like side of a mountain. Keep a watch for a vehicle that he may have used and left behind."

They all got into the shuttle and began their search.

On a radius of about fifteen miles they circled and in no time spotted an abandoned vehicle, half buried in the sand.

"Well done Alex, land the shuttle close to it, must have been abandoned by Joshua, his remains must be inside or nearby." Jim said.

They also spotted a cave, "Perhaps that is the one Joshua was referring to. First we check the vehicle."

They began with the arduous job of shoveling away the sand. Jim got in, and checked the inside. It was clean as widows were shut and no trace of Joshua or his belongings. He pressed the start button. The dash board light came on but the engine was dead. On a panel it indicated 'terminal in box C – 9 dysfunction'. On checking the terminal it was swathed with black mesh like substance.

"The vehicle is powered by solar energy, easy to clean the terminals with a solvent and the vehicle will be functional." Jim said.

They walked up to the cave and entered. Smooth walls, very hard to scrape off any samples just as Joshua had described it. Disappointed and exhausted the crew returned to the Habitat. Early the next day, one of the astronauts, Annie got up and did some chores in the kitchen and prepared coffee. She hammered on a tray and went around to wake the rest. "Wake up you lazy bones," she kept repeating.

"What's the idea, can't you leave us to get some more shut eye," Alex complained.

"Coffee is ready, don't you want Jim to continue with the diary anecdote, wake him up too," Annie said and walked to the kitchen and brought four mugs of steaming coffee. After breakfast they assembled and Jim flipped over the pages to find the pen marker.

"We stopped here where it says, 'To you my diary........," he murmured the rest of the line, "Here we are," and continued reading. "I got up early, had breakfast, got into my space suite, stopped at the graves of my two colleagues and paid silence respect. Checked the tool box, got into the vehicle and drove to the mysterious cave which got me into mindboggling possibilities. I spent the whole morning and afternoon looking for clues to the type of material used to lace the walls so smoothly, found none. I sat on a portable stool which I brought along and was lost in thought. Looked at the floor, sandy with some small stones strewn randomly all over. Must have been the wind that brought in this mess. I decided to check the floor below the sand, was it of the same material as the walls?

"My curiosity kindled, to dig in and find out. I made a hole about two feet wide, and kept digging till finally hit bottom, at about four feet. It was hard, none of my tools could penetrate it. It was clear that it was made of the same material as the walls. That added more fuel to my imagination, certainty all this is not a natural formation, must have been done by some kind of intelligent beings. But who? Certainly not by humans because the only humans who set foot on this planet were dead within days of their arrival and the other is me. With that I packed up and returned to the habitat. Spent many hours thinking.'

'Dear diary, October 13, let me hope the number thirteen is a lucky one for me. It could go the other way, unlucky and meet with my destiny which is obvious. Nervously I am putting these lines as an epitaph, have to get to the bottom of this mystery, can't write anymore, will do so if I return back this evening.'

"Dear diary, it is only three hour since I left this morning and I am back with the most fantastic and unbelievable story. I am writing it down as the day started.

"I left the Habitat at eight in the morning, got into my vehicle and drove straight to the cave. As I got off and began to approach the cave, heard a rumbling sound. I stopped and looked around, could see nothing. When I entered I was greeted by an opening in the wall. I almost fainted. It was a small door and that sound I heard earlier must have been as it slid open. Who or what will be on the other side. I remembered what I wrote earlier, about cannibal entities, I began to shiver in my suit and with a pick axe in hand I moved forward cautiously. At the door I stopped and looked in. It was dark. I stepped in and a little further in, the door began to slide shut. I panicked and wanted to get out. A gentle soft spoken voice greeted me.

"'Welcome Earth man, no harm will come to you.'" It was dark, could see no one, I heard the voice within my headgear, I was terrified.

"Who are you and what you want with me, I can't see anything it is very dark" 'I said nervously.

"Stay calm, you may not like my looks, be prepared to accept my features, I will describe to you our body structure so that you will have an idea what we look like. Most important of all we are a peaceful race and will do you no harm."

"With those comforting words, I became calm and somewhat relaxed. No anxiety, and prepared to face a real alien from a different world.

"Light began to gradually come on, exposing the surroundings what looked like a hall. From a distance a form began to appear walking towards me. It was bipedal. As it came closer I could see a head and on either side of its body a pair of limbs like arms, all four waving in greetings. I reciprocated nervously and soon he, with all four hugged me. I was relieved with that welcoming gesture. His description of himself earlier was rather vague but gave me a rough idea of what to expect.

"For the records, his face oval, large rounded black eyes with no visible iris or pupil, small nose under which a slit for a mouth with no lips. A big round chest, from each side a pair of long arms with hands having three long fingers and a thumb in each palm, a bit of a stomach and two thin legs with feet. I could not guess the gender. The dress was skin tight from head to toe except around the face. Our conversation was very brief. He spoke in clear good English. He said that he had been watching me and was sad the other astronauts had died in an accident. Knowing my condition, he suggested to meet the next day to tell me what he has in store for me. What he said was ambiguous. Before I could say anything, he asked me to leave. 'Try to be early in the morning tomorrow, good bye.' The door slid open and I walked out more confused than when I had walked in.'"

Alex interrupted, "I can imagine his state of mind. Meeting a lifeform on a dead planet, which looks like some over grown insect and talks in English. I am sure he must have hallucinated it all, being under stress and longing for company."

Paula cut in, "I tend to believe in what he has entered in his diary. The way he described the creature that met him was more or less detailed, he could have fantasised something more human or reptilian looking than an over grown insect. Living in Martian condition, the only possibility is an insect. On Earth after the dinosaur extinction, insects survived, why not on Mars."

"You have a point Paula, but for now let us get down to finish reading the diary, he may have said more about them." Jim said and began to read.

"In my Habitat I sat for long hours thinking. I came to a conclusion, it all must have been an illusion, a wishful thinking, when under stress one begins to imagine things to suit apprehensions to satisfy hidden desire. There was no door and no creature that welcomed me and asked me to return the next day. Just for the records if ever anyone reads these pages, and there are no more entries, it would only mean that I have gone back to the cave and walked through that door. Then I would proudly say, "I am not alone or better still, we humans are not alone. If life can exist on this dead world what wonders might be stored out there in the universe. With those comforting words I bid thee good night dear diary."

Jim looked up at his stunned audience and sadly said closing the book, "The rest of the pages are blank, that was his last entry. We can only guess what had happened to him. He did go back, his abandoned vehicle was found outside the cave which confirms that. But cannot say for sure if he met his host. We will never know."

"Shouldn't we survey the area once more, check every inch of that cave for any clues, if we find nothing, give up and consider him missing." Paula observed.

"A good idea, we will do that tomorrow if it takes us the whole day, but if our finding is negative, we will consider Joshua as missing and abandon the search. We have a lot to do before our time runs out, to return to the ship and head for home," Jim instructed.

The next day they combed the path to the cave from where the abandoned vehicle was, inside the cave they checked the walls for any possible indications of a doorway, none was found. They gave up, made a full entry of their conclusions and attached it to Joshua's diary.

"People on Earth will be thrilled to read it, perhaps will be a best seller," Annie commented.

CHAPTER 3

Joshua was the captain of Mars − 1, the first manned mission to land on the planet with two other astronauts five years ago. Misfortune struck when two of them died in a freak storm. His contact with a Martian left him in a dilemma.

At first, Joshua thought he was hallucinating that he met an alien which looked like an overgrown ant. Perhaps one develops sympathetic comfort to believe in what the imagination wants to convey, determined he decided to check it out, go to the cave and prove that he was right. But deep inside him, his senses dictated otherwise. He felt from his host's conversation that he was inviting him, better than face certain death living outside. With that in mind, knowing he might not return to the Habitat, collected all his and dead colleagues belongings and left for the cave. As promised by the alien, the next day when Joshua arrived the door was open and he confidently walked in.

"Welcome Earthman, I was not sure you would return, you have made a good decision, out there you will not survive for long. Make this your home. When I close the door it will not open again, so decide now if you want to stay?" The alien said and waited for his guest to reply. Joshua had to make a decision, thought for a long minute. "Ant looking or whatever, it is better than being out there alone." He uttered one word, "Stay."

"Good, for your convenience, remove your head gear, you will not need it in here, instead put this one on, I will help you with it."

Joshua did as instructed, his companion placed a facial mask with a skull cap that fitted perfectly. From it a thin tube connected to a small pack placed on his shoulders.

"For now you have to wear the mask until such time your system becomes adjusted to our air. Also you will not need this cumbersome suit you are wearing, a simpler tight fit attire would do the job. You can change into it once we get to your accommodation."

They walked through a long corridor with lights shining bright, Joshua looked up and down at the clean environment and shining pathway, "Your people have made this?"

"All in good time will be explained to you," Was his companion's answer.

They entered a little kiosk and his companion pressed a button. Second later emerged into a large open area where many of his kind bustling around not paying attention to the odd looking entity in their midst.

"As long as I am with you they know you are special, and in due course when they get to know you they will be your friends. Now look up, this is hollowed cavity, the crust is above us, we are hundreds of feet below the surface and in that wall we live, apartments are dung into it, all connected by a common passageway. Below we have our workshops and machines that give us light, refined air to breath and water filtration units. On our right is an underground lake that stretches for miles. There are many such water pockets some as big as an ocean, drinkable after some refining."

While walking around, engaged in conversation, suddenly there was an alarm, a loud buzzing sound, Joshua's companion froze where he stood and so did all the individuals in the area. Then with a collective instant impulse they began to sprint towards the entrance of their mountain wall habitats. His companion grabbed his hand and asked him to follow him.

"What is the commotion about?" I asked as we hurried to the entrance in the wall.

"Not now, we have to take shelter from the water creatures, they are bad, they like to eat us.

"Who are the water creatures, and where do they come from?"

"Don't ask questions now, I'll explain it to you in due course. Once the gates are shut we are safe,"

Shortly after, there was another buzzing sound with a different tone.

"With the doors and windows shut the sound is fainter but audible, it sounds more pleasant to our ears than the first, but deadly to the water creatures, it makes them disoriented and confused. They rush back to the water and disappear. They are a nuisance but soon help will come to permanently eradicate them or find a solution to house them elsewhere." The companion explained.

Joshua wanted to ask what and whose help would be coming, his mind was churning with questions but abstained to ask as the reply he would get from his companion, 'all in good time your queries will be answered.'

They got into an elevator, got off and walked through corridors and entered a small room. "This is where you will stay......." Before his companion could finish his sentence Joshua showed an uncomfortable feeling about the room, no bed, kitchen or the amenities of living conditions.

"Don't look disappointed I have not finished explaining, when you press this button," pointing to a little dent in the wall, "Gently put a little pressure, a door will slide open."

They entered a large room with tables and chairs at one corner, a pantry with all that one needs in a kitchen. Adjoining was another small room with a single bed and a closet, a chair and a table.

"I hope you approve, it is the best we can offer, and one more thing, once you shut your door no one can enter unless you press this button next to the door on the inside. Now you rest and when you feel the bed vibrate gently with music coming through a speaker it will wake you up to get ready. A machine in your pantry will prepare your breakfast by selecting from the menu on the wall, same for other meals. I will come after ten hours of your time and take you to meet the Elders." Before he could ask who the Elders were, his companion left.

Joshua was hungry, in the pantry the menu was in English, "Was that room prepared for me or some other from Earth, but no humans ever came to Mars before us three astronauts, two are dead and only me alive. Perhaps tomorrow I will have some answers." With those thoughts, had his meal and went to bed.

CHAPTER 4

The bed gently shook and vibrated, Joshua opened his eye and jumped up, his first thought was a quake, the sound of music brought him to his senses, sat back on the bed pondering.

He had breakfast and waited for his companion to come.

The companion arrived, the door opened and he walked in. Surprised, Joshua said, "I thought no one can enter without my allowing to do so."

"Only I am authorised to enter any apartment, a privileged position. Now it is time to go and meet the Elders."

"Who are the Elders?"

"Soon you will meet them and they will explain."

They walked through a narrow corridor and got into an elevator, got off into what looked like a large room with a few of their kind standing by. They were ushered to an adjoining room and left alone. "We are at the top of this complex, where the Elders reside." His companion explained.

A door opened, "Let us enter, the Elders are waiting for us."

On the far end of the room, five similar in looks as his companion sat at a rectangular table, all looked alike with no indication of age or sex.

As they entered one of them addressed him softly, "Welcome Earthman, what is your name?"

"Joshua."

"Jooshhwa," An Elder said with some difficulty in pronouncing.

"No, Josh-wa," he replied breaking the letters into two syllables.

"Please sit down Josh-wa, you too Akak."

"So that is my companion's name, Akak," Joshua said to himself.

"Josh-wa we are very happy that you made the right decision to stay with us, Akak will teach you about our simple rules and feel free to do as you please. We do not look human, but in time you will get used to it. Our species are much older than you humans. We have survived the changes of our world from what it was to what it is today. It is a long story. A few lessons with the teachers will explain how it all happened. By the way the teachers are not from our species they come from another world, they have a lot of resembles to your kind. You will enjoy their company."

Joshua was listening attentively at the same time trying to digest the idea of another life- form similar to humans. "Who are they?"

"All in good time, you just concentrate on what I am telling you."

Another thought, "They too can read my mind,"

"Yes among ourselves we communicate telepathically, now to continue what I was talking about." One of the elders said, "Those human like friends came to our world many years ago and found us in a degenerated state. Our infrastructures were dwindling to irreparable level, they helped us to reconstruct our passageways, living condition and all what you see here.

"They come and go, keep an eye on us, but there is one thing they haven't been able to outdo. There is a lurking danger in our waters, the creatures look similar to your manatee, with six limbs like an octopus, a long tongue, and can change their shape to anything they attach to. They waits for their pray and with a lash of the tongue which extends to about five feet, rope their victims and tear their limbs to shreds with their powerful tentacles and swallow them whole. They lives in our water, come out often to feed on us. Their only weakness is the sound of a certain frequency, which makes their limbs become dysfunctional and harmless.

"Our friends will come someday to take them away to Jupiter's moon Europa where below the ice there is an ocean, booming with microbial and lower form of life like in our waters. They also promised to change the climatic condition of this world to make it habitable to their form of life and perhaps to you humans. It has been many years since they began working on this project. We have been told it is progressing satisfactorily. Once you spend some time with the teachers, you will learn more about this world. Any questions?" The Elder concluded.

"Just one. How did you learn to speak my language?" Joshua asked.

"From the teachers, they taught us many languages and the history of your and their world, how they live and the variety of higher and lower forms of life. You will be surprised to know that some thousands of years ago they tried to acclimatized some of us to breathe the Earth air, took us to places like Turkey, the Grand Canyon in the United States and some other places, but soon had to return as the climate was not too comfortable for us. Perhaps there are still some traces of our living quarters on hill sides which look like a mesh. You feel at home, Akak will be with you for some time until you become more familiar with our life style. You will enjoy the company of the teachers. We will meet again, have a pleasant day."

Joshua and Akak left. At his quarters, Joshua said, "I am so glad, don't have to wear a space suite in here except this tight fit dress, but wearing the mask to breathe your air is inconvenient. Hopefully will not need it as in time I will get adjusted to the conditions in here. What about your teachers, do they need these.

"The teachers have been here for a long time, taking a certain herb helped them to breathe our air. You too, will adapt in due course. It is not much different from the atmosphere on your planet. Tomorrow we meet the teachers."

The next day they visited them, to Joshua they looked human and they did not tell him that they were from Urna.

"Can't believe it, how can you not be human when you look like me?" Joshua exclaimed.

"True, but we come from another world, the universe has many surprises. Soon some of them will be told to you. At present it is premature. Feel free to come at any time and use our library." One of the teachers offered.

CHAPTER 5

Ashtok with worried concern was discussing with Ayond the situation on Earth. The Guardian had informed him, in a number of countries localised hooliganism had erupted, in the Middle East, South Asia and Africa. "As it is within their borders, he could do nothing, the local authorities were doing their best to control the situation. But the most disturbing news was that one Middle East nation has been secretly using an underground facility, doing something worth investigating. It is not detectable as it is located in the desert covered by sand dunes. By sheer accident a satellite picked up a camel caravan plodding across the desert and suddenly vanishing. Days later, a tent was spotted in that location, from under it some vehicles emerged, maneuvered through the dunes and got on to a road. The Guardian's suspicion arose and sent agents dressed as Bedouin nomads to pass by that spot. From a well camouflaged lookout post under the sand, security men sprang, searched their belongings and considering their shabby appearance were allowed to go. The Guardian is keeping a watch."

"What is he going to do about it?" Ayond asked.

"Nothing for the time being, in the meantime he will collect as much details as possible on the site and find out if it is a prison or some other activity is going on. Also if a foreign nation is involved. Only then we can take action if necessary." He said and proudly announced, "In two months my specially designed ship will be ready, you and your Earth colleagues will join me on the inaugural flight, and enjoy the comforts of a home and the safety of a fortress."

"Where will we be going?"

"A brief tour of the outer part of the solar system."

"What about your Mars project?"

"That is in good hands of our technicians. The trip will be short, two weeks at the most, consider it a little vacation."

Meanwhile, the Guardian busied himself with collecting data on the suspicious desert facility site. It was too risky to send more agents. He decided to fly using a small invisible craft. Hovering above, took pictures and sonar readings which displayed a gigantic cavity about three hundred feet in diameter, commonly found in desert locations. Water collects underground, used up over the years and eventually dries up. Such cavities are often made prisons for political and senior personalities who would never see the light of day again. He spotted a tent and a few camels, a man busied cooking and two children running around, perhaps a setup to throw away any suspicion. A pickup truck drove up, the ground opened and it drove through. Late that night several trucks went in and later a bus came out. He had to find a way to get in, but how, the place was monitored by heavy security.

Only a few in the hierarchy of the government of that country knew what went on inside. Within that cavity was a well organised factory engaged in the manufacture of nuclear weapons. The man in charge sat high in a glass room with television monitors displaying all what went on within.

Two men dressed in white overalls, the rest in light gray. The two in white were foreigners, James Goldberg an American and the other Uri Lennov, a Russian, the rest were locals. Both scientists were kidnapped and made to work against their will to develop the deadly armament. Both were told, after the completion of their task each will receive five million dollars, already deposited in their names in a Swiss bank, but will be released once they complete the project and will be freed from custody and safely at home.

Microphones were stitched on their clothes, all what they say was recorded and analysed. Supervisors followed every move they made, there was no room for errors or acts of sabotage. They were housed within the facility and were given the comforts of living in a luxury apartment, but going outside was not allowed. The two scientist did their job diligently and were appraised.

It has been two years since their abduction. For their good behaviour security conditions became less restrictive. Once a month on a weekend they were taken to a hotel where they could relax. But leaving the facility they had to have a disguise. They were told to grow their facial and head hair and at the hotel not to speak to anyone. Both acted their part well. Six months later they were allowed two weekends. Two security men chaperoned their every move. Most of the time the same security men accompanied and could predict exactly their routine activity, go for a dip in the indoor swimming pool in the morning and another dip late afternoon in the outdoor pool not far from the main entrance to the hotel. On one such trip while fully stretched in their bathing trunks next to the outdoor pool Uri said something in an undertone while staring up at the late afternoon sky.

"It is all wrong what we are doing."

Knowing they were in their bathing trunks and no one could listen, James asked Uri to repeat what he had said. Uri repeated.

"Uri we are prisoners with a salary, can't do anything, they know every move we make and hear every word we speak, except in this attire."

"I was thinking, what if we continue to do our work industriously at the same time disable the bombs from becoming active," Uri said turning over laying on his stomach.

"Good idea, but not practicable, unless you have a way to do it." James said turning over resting his arms below his head.

"Yes I can. Connect all leads on the missiles to show on their systems their readiness but have a weak bypass connection to the main terminals that will not carry the circuit for detonation, disabling them. Only on one I can do a trick, put a timer to explode on a particular date, it will go off within the premises and blow the entire desert facility to kingdom come. It is fool proof, I have experimented it back home."

"And we perish with them, no sir, I want to live," James was not pleased.

"Of course we will not perish with them, I have a plan to escape."

"Escape? Impossible, with all that security you cannot get out of that hole we are in.'

"It will be on a timer, I will set it to go off on a particular day, before that we will be free and safe many miles away. It will be set when we are hundred percent ready with our plan."

"How do you propose our escape, with all those guards?"

"On a weekend stay at the hotel, after dinner we have a casual walk outside as we have been doing in the past, get into a car which I will arrange through Rent a Car service which will be left near the entrance, get into it and head for the city and get asylum in my or your embassy. The embassy will gladly put us in a helicopter and ferry us to one of their war ships in the area."

"That's is a tall order, what if we fail?"

"The risk is there, but worth a try, we will be doing the world a favour. Think about it."

Soon the plan was set into motion. Having gained the confidence of the overall watchful eyes by routinely sticking to how to spend their leisure hours on weekends at the hotel, James and Uri got to work. For several weekends they repeated the drill, window shopped within the hotel, strolled before and after dinner. Had a dip in the pool before retiring for the night. The security men got used to their routine and could predict exactly all their moves.

The time was ripe to act. All the nuclear devises were disabled except one. The timer was set to go off at midday fourteen days later. It was a Thursday, ready to be driven by the security guards to the hotel for the weekend.

That afternoon was exceptionally hot, they decided to take a dip in the outdoor pool. It was crowded with families and kids, they played with them and spent the afternoon leisurely. The watchful eyes monitoring them were getting bored. They sat not too far from them and sipped tea one cup after another. James and Uri watched their chaperons discretely.

After a while they went to the dressing room to change. Came out merrily whistling, as they passed by the guards waved a hand in greeting with no reciprocal gesture. Before entering the hotel they looked back and saw them still sitting almost motionless and uninterested.

At the cafeteria they ordered tea. Suddenly the apparition of the two guards materialized beside them. "Had a good swim? It is very hot today, we almost went to sleep watching you two. Enjoy our hospitality, you are nice people," One of the guards said.

"Why don't you join us for a cup of tea?" James offered.

"Thank you, already had too many cups, we will leave you alone and before I forget, please wear your night coats when you go to bed, last week one of you slept without it and had to be woken up, you know the rules." He said and both left the cafeteria.

"With those mikes attached they want to hear our snores." Uri said and added, "Let's move out before the shops close, we have to do some shopping."

Lazily they drifted along the corridors window shopping, stopping at a boutique. They entered, looked around leisurely, picked up shirts with exquisite designs and placed them across their chests, "How do I look in this one?" James asked Uri who had one across his.

"You look great James" Uri said. They spent time bargaining when Uri nudged James by his elbow drawing his attention to the guards who were watching them through the show case window.

When they left the shop, James approached the guards and in a typical American style displayed what he had bought with a bit of humour.

"Do you like it? See how it looks on me." James removed his shirt, tucked it randomly into a shopping bag he was carrying and put on the boutique shirt.

"Uri try yours."

Soon both displayed their colourful attires with a bit of theatrical display.

One of the security guards said to the other in Arabic, "These crazy foreigners, sometime they act like children. Let them enjoy their weekend."

Seeing some spectators gathering to witness the show, the guards moved on to save an embarrassing situation. Uri stopped at the Car Rental, and headed for the display rack of post cards. Both took their time in perusing through them.

"Look at these card, they are wonderful, I must buy a few to remind me of this great country." Uri said aloud for the guards to hear as they stood not far from them.

They continued to talk loud and show their admiration, sometimes joking and sometimes with serious expressions.

The security seeing their innocent gestures ignored them and walked away. There was no visible danger in leaving them alone, at least they thought.

Seeing them disappear, Uri casually said to James, "That was clever, to take off our shirts with microphones and put these on, they did not even suspect it. You have tucked them well in that shopping bag, no one can hear a thing."

A man from the shop came out to encourage and help them with their selection of cards. While engrossed in his sales talk, Uri casually said, "Can we rent a car for three days to visit some of the nearby places."

"Why not, that will cost you, in U.S. dollars seventy five per day with a full tank of petrol. After that you have to put more at your cost. When do you want to pick it up?"

"As we intend to leave very early tomorrow morning and it being a Friday your shop will not open until after your afternoon prayer, how about leaving the car at the far end of the drive near the main entrance of the hotel before you close for the night."

Quickly Uri took out the money and paid him. The man went into the shop and from a rack with many keys took out one and handed it to Uri.

"It is a brown Mazda. New car, look after it well. I will drive it to the location you asked me and park it there. I have a duplicate key." The car rental man said.

No sooner the deal was done they left the shop casually, merrily ambled through the corridors and entered the dining room.

They lingered a little longer, enjoying a three course meal, followed by dessert and coffee, still in their newly bought shirts. They stepped outside as they had always done in the past. It was a routine drill to walk up and down the beautifully manicured lawns and settle on a bench next to the pool. The security guards sat at a distance, watching. An hour later, the security guards were bored and tired, reclined on their chairs, watching over them was a formality and a routine knowing what would come next.

James and Uri saw the car-rental man drive the car near the main gate entrance. To avoid any contact with him, they looked the other way and busied themselves removing their shirts and jumped into the pool in their shorts.

As they always did for months to tune the guards to a simple routine, swam two lengths, stopped and chatted at one end. They noticed the guards stand up and disappear into the hotel, "Now is our chance, they must have gone in for a bite." James said as they raced to get out. They grabbed their shirts and with large strides raced for the waiting car. Looked back at the spot where the guards sat, there was no sign of them. They got into the car and drove off, at first gently and after a few more feet, took off.

They were on the main highway, forty minutes later they were at the gate of the United States embassy. It took some time to enter after some formalities, they were escorted to a room where security personnel verified their identities. They told their story and soon were ferried to a war ship in the area. Helicopters leave and land within the embassy is a routine drill and no suspicion were aroused.

The security chaperons at the hotel raised an alarm to their headquarters but were too late to apprehend the fugitive scientists.

A complete search of the underground facility was made and found all in order. They had a complete functional arsenal, so they thought.

The Russian and United States embassies contacted their friendly nations' counterparts, and discreetly evacuated their personal and waited for the scheduled big bang. Their governments informed the Guardian, the head of the New World Order.

As planned, two weeks later a nuclear explosion carved a crater miles wide, sending tons of sand into the air obstructing the sun light for days. A local television station announced 'A terrible accident at one of our military bases, cause of the explosion is unknown, investigations are going on.' The broadcast played it down as if nothing serious had occurred.

"Playing with fire, their evil intentions payed them back in kind." The Guardian said to Ashtok.

Ashtok just remarked, "Good for those who want to play with fire."

CHAPTER 6

Ashtok proudly led Ayond and her earth team to a hanger where his newly constructed gilded coloured and streamlined body space ship stood majestically. It was like no other, three hundred feet in length and fifty feet wide. The front tapered to a pointed shaft and the aft a ring in which it housed what looked like rocket boosters.

Ashtok said pointing to the ship, "It is finally ready, and as promised we will go and have a test run. Before that, let me show you the inside." They entered the hold section, "In here I have small crafts." They moved to two upper decks, for storage and staff accommodation. The third level had guest suites and entertainment facilities.

"Very impressive, facilities of a luxury ocean liner, only that we are going sailing into empty space." Jim commented.

"You are right and wrong, we will be travelling through space and see the wonders of some of the worlds in our solar system, in one we will dive through its atmosphere and float around, feel what it is like." Ashtok said.

"That would be a life-time experience, what a privilege." Sam commented.

"Such a trip will take us months if not years." David remarked.

"Not so David," Ashtok replied, "With the speed this ship is capable of, will take us less than two weeks to the furthest point we plan to go and return to Urna."

"Which is to what planet?" David asked.

"Pluto." Ashtok said and suggested to go to their suites and refresh. "Once ready, an attendant will escort all to the flight-deck where you will be comfortably seated." Shortly after, on the flight deck they moved around like tourists admiring its configuration. Semicircular in shape with widows and chairs all around. In the front a control panel of instruments with different gadgets and devices, small screens and numerous tiny coloured lights continuously blinking. There were four chairs, two crew members sat at the two ends, the two in the middle were empty.

Ashtok made an announcement, "Sit wherever you wish, the seats will secure you automatically and release when it is safe to move around. Ayond will sit with me at the controls. I will teach her how to fly this beautiful machine."

They were seated in pairs near each window. Ashtok at the controls, swirled his chair and looked at his passengers. Said to Ayond sitting beside him, "Look at them, David, Saeed, Sam, Aishtra, Daniel, Fiona, Jim and his wife, the good people from Earth, proud of them for being with us on our world and will share the joy of being the first humans to travel that far into the solar system."

Through a microphone Ashtok spoke, "Ladies and gentlemen, during the journey I will keep updating you, you can talk to me naturally from your seats they have microphones in them, you have to press the little button on your armrest to do so. Our trip will take us to the Jovian planets, starting with Saturn, all the way to Uranus and then to Neptune where we will dive into it, then hop over to Pluto and on the journey back visit our neighbour Jupiter and some of its moons. Now be ready for the takeoff."

Ayond said softly to Ashtok, "It was good of you to mention Aishtra, though she is of a different species but also from Earth as our human friends."

"Without doubt, after all she is married to Sam, a human," after a pause he added, "I wonder what category of species their children will be." He came back on the microphone, "Initially we'll be travelling at a very high speed, it will be some hours, recline your seats if you want to have a nap. Meals will be served to you in the comfort of your chairs."

The takeoff was smooth, no engine sound or any vibrations, they sailed through the emptiness of space and many hours later reached Saturn, flew above its rings and circled them. Visited its moons Enceladus and Titan, flew closer to its surface, saw the splendour of its topography and molten methane lakes.

On the speaker Ashtok explained, "The site down there on Titan; Earth may have looked like this billions of years ago. That methane and hydrocarbons may have been the source of your crude oil which you people wrongly refer to as fossil fuel. Aishtra, was it not during those conditions the Jinn species evolved? I have to sit with your king someday and learn about the chemistry how you developed."

Next stop was to the knocked over Uranus. During that journey
they went to their suites, slept, refreshed and enjoyed watching
a movie. After a hearty meal they returned to the flight deck to
witness the approaching gas giant. After orbiting it, visited some
of its moons. Next was Neptune. Again the same drill to pass their
time. The hours passed quickly as they had plenty to entertain
them. The colossal blue sphere of Neptune was breathtaking.
Their speed slowed. Ashtok announced, "Soon we will have a dip
into its atmosphere, sit tight and enjoy the scene." The cabin lights
were dimmed and powerful lights on the outside flooded the blue
haze of the planet's vaporous aether as the ship plunged into it.
Blue all around them, unexpectedly, from below, appeared rising
upwards, strange threadlike white spiral formations. The scene
was awesome. Deeper into its enigmatic atmosphere the spirals
were all over, coming in contact with the ship. "You can hear the
impacts, the outer sensors transmit it to the speakers." Ashtok
explained. The crackling sound increased, filled the cabin like
hail particles storming. More appeared. "I think we had enough of
them, it is better to surface and heading for the last outpost, Pluto.'
Ashtok said, then added, "Our trip would not be complete without
visiting it. It will be long before reaching it, I suggest go to your
suites and relax. I will send for you when our approach begins."

They returned to witness a small rocky planetoid, very different
from its gas giants. The ship encircled it twice, north to south and
east to west. Ashtok commented, "There is something inscrutable
about this mysterious world, someday I shall come back to explore
it in detail. I have a strong hunch that I will find something that
no one can imagine in their wildest dreams. Perhaps a new *form
of 'existence'*, stationary but capable of communicating by thought
transfer, telepathically."

"Stationary like what, only protruding rocks, this world is more than three billion miles from the sun, and if any gases exist, must be frozen solid." David said on the microphone.

"True," Ashtok replied, "It might appear so, but I have some wild assumptions, it is a kind of a hobby. If you wish, we can plan another trip, exclusively to explore Pluto, I may find what my instincts tell me and may change our understanding of the universe. But this has to wait till after I complete my mission on Mars."

As scheduled, on their return journey, before reaching Jupiter, visited some of its moons. Calisto, the second largest, then Ganymede, the largest which has plenty of water trapped below its surface as in Europa. They orbited Europa, Ashtok commented, "Sometime soon we will visit and explore its waters, connected with my Mars mission. Will explain it to you later. Now we are approaching our closest neighbour, Io the third largest of Jupiter's moons and if you remember, it was the home of that evil creature Xanthum, you were with Ayond when she exterminated him along with his entire race some years ago." (vii) Shortly after their journey come to an end, "Go home and reflect." He added. True to his word they were back on Urna late evening on the fourteenth day.

As they left the ship, Sam commented, "Can't imagine we have travelled millions of miles in a short time, what an experience."

"Space travel has to be conquered further, to make it possible to visit other worlds within a reasonable distance say between one to a hundred parsecs," Ashtok said.

"You lost me, what does that means in simple English," Sam asked.

"Simply consider it as a measure of distance outside the solar system. One parsec is just over 3.2 light years and 100 parsecs is about 300 light years. That would be the beginning, truly speaking, to achieve a capability to travel to our neighbour, the Andromeda Galaxy which is about 8000 parsecs would be just perfect. But within the solar system, Astronomical Unit or AU is used to measure distances, it stands for the distance of the Earth from the sun which is 93 million miles. Earth is one AU from the sun and Mars is about 1.54 AU, Pluto is nearly 40 astronomical units. It will be the day when we can master space travel beyond our present capability. Nothing is impossible. Now go home and relax, we will meet in a few days. I have something important to discuss.

That night Ayond sat in her study reminiscing the past years as how her team came to be and labeled by her, after their escapades on Earth finding a medallion left behind by her alien predecessors with a trusted person, some nine hundred years ago and their search to retrieve a devise with which it could read a message left by them to tell the world of their presence and contribution to their welfare. She remembered how the message was received when read at the United Nations. The members took it as a prank or a western concocted trick. Even some of the super powers did not pay much attention to it. She recollected the words of someone who spoke hotly, "An alien race on our planet all these years, and we did not hear of them. Only the British government confirms their existence, why did they not share it with us and now they want us to believe in this fictional story. Is it some kind of a joke or some sort of a conspiracy? No thank you." Those words still rang in her ears.

"It was a wise decision to leave the humans to solve their problems, and we are happy to have my earthly friends who came with us. They are well settled and form a part of our community. Ashtok and the Guardian are equally happy with them." (viii) With those recollections she smiled and said to herself, "Those were difficult days, at the same time my happiest."

As requested by Ashtok, they all met at Ayond's place a few days later and waited for him to arrive. He entered, with a sporty gesture of his hand said, "Sorry I am late, on my way I found a baby bird on the road, fallen from its nest, had to put it back where it belonged. Now before we start, how about some of your weeds you call tea that will refresh me to think clearer," he said with a bit of humour. (ix)

"You are insulting one of nature's great marvels, we don't call it weeds, you can say shoots or sprouts or leaves for those who relish it in that form, being a machine you don't know what you are missing, forgive the expression not being impertinent."

Soon tea pots and cups with exquisite flower designs decorated the table and in front of Ashtok a large plate with stems and in a small plate loose tea leaves sprinkled with mint. "You will find the mint an added blend to enhance the taste and aroma," Ayond put in.

While all sipped in silence, Ashtok busied himself with sniffing and chewing and discretely removing it from his mouth. "My mental receptors are fully charged by your wonder refresher," He looked up and said, "Ladies and gentlemen thank you for coming, you must have recovered from our brief tour of the far side of the solar system. It must have been quite educational. Now to get down to business, I want to have your views on a serious topic concerning your home planet. My decision will come into effect only if you all, yes I mean each one of you agree." He paused for a little while then gently asked Aishtra and Fiona to come forward.

"Both of you represent two distinct species on Earth, come and sit by my sides." Looking at the others he added. "Earthmen what do you see?"

"Seeing you sandwiched between two flowers!" Jim exclaimed.

"Well said Jim, if your world can produce such flowers why do you like to pluck and step on them. Here we have two different species from your world, Aishtra a Jinn, Fiona a human, they love and respect each other, and none of them wants to harm the other. Down there on your planet people of the *same species* are at each other's throat. We have lived there long enough to understand the reasons for the hatred, racial discrimination, and wars. A line drawn on a map separates two peoples, each wants to be separate from the other. In some cases to the extent of exterminating the other. In the old days wars were fought on open grounds, lasts for a day or two. Then conflicts took another form, nations took sides bringing misery and suffering to millions. Today, there is a new kind of challenge with a weapon most dangerous; called money and money talks. Its language has many dialects, translated into achieving different functions, one of them is *giving*, can be donations or gratuities. Generously flow to capture the unsuspecting weaker minds to spread chaos and confusion, not localised but creeps into wider areas bringing suffering to the innocent. The whole of humanity become confused and roped into proxy battles. The initiators are happy to achieve their goals, not knowing sooner or later they will inherit what they have sown.

"Money talks loud and the mighty bows, a whisper can do wonders to satisfy the whisperer. That is one side of the coin, the other, monetary offerings help to lubricate the entrance of disrupting ideas to weak poor nations to control their naïve masses adherence and pave the way for the donator to achieve a sphere of influence to spread chaos as and when required.

"Religions on the other hand are meant to be a tool to be good. I have seen its development from the start, in different lands, different concepts, just a few were truly pacific, spread peacefully and did not go to wars. In the case of some, sad to say, it was not the case, was corrupted by the hands of scruples, bigoted self-styled so called, men of god. Millions have suffered by their treacherous and merciless hands for thousands of years. Who are they to judge others by their God's commandments? The pages of history are full of such atrocities, millions have suffered, such records will not be erased, once written cannot be delated.

I am reminded of a quatrain by Omar Khayyam the Persian poet:

'The moving finger writes; and, having writ,
Moves on: nor all thy Piety nor Wit
Shall lure it back to cancel half a line
Nor all thy Tears wash out a Word of it.'

"It says it all, humanity will not forget what has been done. In this day and age there is no reason or justification to behave and live with those archaic dogmas, those who wish to live in that style should do so on their own, not force it down the throat of others. Most civilized people have come out of it but there is still that minuscule remnant which can pollute the rest, like the old adage 'one bad apple can spoil the rest'.

"With that I want you all to sit and think, in a few days we'll meet again and I want a unanimous verdict how to solve this problem *once* and for all." Ashtok stressed on the word once.

Solemnly they departed with a gentle and respectable departing gesture. From there they met at David's home. For several long minutes no one spoke.

David with a low grave voice broke the silence, "We have a tough decision to make. Ashtok has clearly indicated a positive line of action subject to our approval. Politics back home is dirty, most leaders put up a face of holier than thou image but deep under full of devious and corrupt schemes. Habits are imbued and not easy to change. How about you Jim, what have you to offer?"

"I agree to what you have said, the powerful and mighty are well protected by their accomplices, any opposition would be silenced. Even with the implementation of the New World Order they have found loop holes to elude the system. Perhaps nothing can change their modus operandi, the only way out is to have a few drastic exemplary actions to put the fear of god."

"You mean severe punishment?" David asked.

"Yes, it may sound crude, but sacrifices have to be made for the sake of future generations."

"What about you Daniel?" David asked.

"I am a man of peace, if that path does not bring in results, I leave it to man to decide his own destiny. History tells us, man has bought about the destruction of millions of his own kind in the name of his king or God. In this modern age the antiquated thinking is still practiced. Let him now reap what he has sown. When you have a bad seed in your basket discard it before it infects the lot. Only then there can be harmony and live in peace like good neighbours. That is my humble opinion."

Fiona raised her hand. "Yes Fiona, you have something to contribute?" David was pleased to hear a woman's point of view.

"Perhaps I am too naive to give an opinion, but having worked with seniors in my capacity as a confidential secretary to the Prime Minister of my country, have seen and learned a lot how the clock ticks. The influence of friendly nations, some of which are small and insignificant but have resources and wealth to influence our foreign policy. We wage wars on their call, the innocent suffer the Middle East is one example. Even the New World Order with the Guardian as the head is no match for the conniving bugs that will eventually erode the woodwork and bring total chaos and doom to the world. Eradicate them before they infect the entire planet."

"Well said Fiona, very strongly put and has a lot of sense. From what I have heard, all are of the same opinion, in a nutshell; remove that bug riddled mattress from underneath you and torch it. I tend to agree though it seems gruesome but years from now, history will tell how correct their forefathers were to cleanse the world.

"Sam and Aishtra, have you any contributions to our thoughts," David addressed them as they sat cuddled on a sofa.

"I don't think we are qualified to give an opinion, we know nothing of politics, you are our senior members, and whatever you and the rest decide is okay with us."

David called Ayond and requested her to join them. Gladly she accepted and minutes later she entered with a bouquet of flowers.

She was greeted with cheerful words. David escorted her to a chair, "You have been our guiding spirit, now we seek your opinion on our decision on what Ashtok requires of us." Pin drop silence filled the room.

"It is hard for me to accept or reject what you all have come up with. Honestly speaking I have no opinion on what is to be done. It is between you all and our Supreme High, Ashtok. I will accept his decisions as the final word," Ayond said politely and to change the subject, added happily, "What has happened to your hospitality, I am thirsty!"

David shouted, "Sam, Can you do the honours."

The partying lasted for hours, Ayond promised to convey to Ashtok their decision.

CHAPTER 7

Ashtok sat with Aishtra and Fiona at his sides. Ayond and the rest took their seats at a long rectangular table facing them.

"Ayond tells me you all have come out with a point of view."

"Yes Ashtok we have, though it is not conclusive but has some elements of what is to be done." David narrated in detail how they felt about the main issue. "There are a few hard liners who actually believe in what they are doing is the right thing, they have followers who tow the line to do their dirty work to control the feeble minded. Of course heavy funding is involved to make them tick to spread their so called doctrine. It is a well-knit network. I can go on for hours, only those who studied and lived in those area and conditions can really understand how their mind works. It is not new, has been since time immemorial. I would consider it a form of racism where divisions and categories are created causing chaos."

"Thank you David, You have said it all. I had made a bit of research on my own. I had instructed the Guardian who is on Earth to contact some of the senior Jinn for their opinion too. After all they are living side by side with humans in their own worldly dimension, can't be seen by humans but the Jinn can, but all the same they are there. He was lucky to meet the king of the

Jinn and what he told him was implausible. The king revealed that when humans emerged on this world, spread anarchy and destruction and ultimately brought destruction and extinction to their kind. Millions of years later when they re-emerged the second time, the Jinn wanted to eliminate them. They knew from their predecessors past performance, they would be no better. Their seniors debated with the idea, but unanimously decided not to, but be given a second chance. The king also said it was a bad decision as humans have inherited the genes of their ancestors and will surely bring their own demise. He agreed to help in any way to save humanity in removing the cancerous tissues plaguing the social order. That was the king of the Jinn's point of view about their human species neighbour. For now let us leave the subject," Ashtok concluded and added, "I have some good news."

All in attendance shuffled in their chairs and readjusted their posture with a gentle grin on their faces.

"In a couple of days I am taking you on a ride to our neighbour Mars. Once we are there I will show you what we have been doing for a very long time with the help of some of the people which in your terminology are called the Martians." The moment the word Mars and Martians were mentioned all were dumbfounded. Ayond and Aishtra just smiled.

Ashtok continued, "Now if you remember in an earlier meeting Ayond mentioned about 'our most treasured secret'; she was referring to the Martians, and secondly about the words, 'just vanished, not in the real sense'; referring again to the Martians having taken away the third astronaut.

"Some time ago two unmanned Earth probes almost detected our activity there and sadly had to be disabled. It is too early for them to know what we are doing. Then there was the first landing mission of three astronauts which was doomed form the start. Two of them died accidently in a freak storm and the third disappeared without a trace. Of course now you know where he is, a Martian guest. Sometime later a second manned mission landed at the location as their fist, to investigate about its failure and search for the missing astronaut. They found nothing, collected a few soil samples and left. I am taking you for an escapade to Mars. You will see our sincere intentions to help all forms of life."

Days later, Ashtok escorted Ayond and her colleagues to the newly designed spaceship they had the pleasure to tour some of the planets on its inaugural flight. On its side beautifully embossed, '*The Gentle Stream*'.

"You did not have a name when we first had the pleasure, and why that name?" Sam asked.

"No particular reason, I just fancied the words, it is most befitting for that configuration," He said casually then added, "For a short time we will be travelling at a high speed as you had experienced earlier when we visited the outer planets."

The Gentle Stream lifted off, higher and higher, it began to move forward, first gently, then a little faster, with a sudden impulse it began to race forward with an unconceivable speed. On the outside the universe seemed to roll pass, stars were like streaks of lights. After a while they retired to their suits and just before reaching the vicinity of Mars, they were escorted back to the flight deck. "We will be passing between the two Martian moons, Phobos and Deimos, those sitting on the right will see one and those on the left the other. We will orbit for some time and enjoy the enigmatic display of the planet's surface features. We will descend in a shuttle, before that put on your space suits, they are more convenient than what your astronauts use. As it is your first time you may feel a bit of discomfort but soon will get used to it." Shortly after they were led to a room, men and women were separated by a curtain.

The attendants undressed them and sprayed each with a blast of warm air. Seconds later turned moist and cool, as it dried gave a constricting sensation. A skin tight fit suit was slipped on from their feet up to the chin, around the back of the head up to the eye brows. Another blast of the warm dry air was administered, the suit began to contract and cling tightly to their skin. "It is just one centimeters thick, made from a special fabric, soon you will not feel its presence as if not wearing anything." The attendant explained. Flexible lightweight facial masks were carefully fitted onto their faces and attached to the suit with a tube connected to a small rectangular box strapped on to the back of their shoulders. The eye coverings were almond shaped with a tinge of gray, the ears, mouth and nose had some paddings which contained hearing aids, microphones and breathing vents. The shoes on their feet were enclosed with a special material that will keep them balanced as the gravity on Mars is less than forty percent that on Earth. They were informed that the suits will protect them from radiation, heat and cold and the little box on their shoulders helps to breathe normally for twenty four hours when a refill is needed.

When they stepped out of the room, Ashtok and Aishtra were waiting. "How about you both, don't need to put on suits?" Sam asked.

"No, I don't. Remember I am a machine. As I said before, there are advantages and disadvantages to be so. Aishtra does not need it too, remember she is a Jinn." Ashtok said and led them to the shuttle.

They boarded and were secured in their seats, the shuttle smoothly slipped out of *The Gentle Stream* and its engines came to life. There was no sound but a slight jolt was felt. The descent to Mars was an experience not to be forgotten, its perplexed topography, all brown, a large black shaded area stretched for miles, the poles generously covered with ice.

David softly murmured, "What a comparison with good old Earth, there we would have been watching the colours of blue, green, white and all shades of brown. A beautiful piece of rock, a Garden of Eden."

Daniel added, "Truly speaking a Garden of Eden, not in the Biblical sense, but metaphorically. The Flora and Fauna, the emergence of intelligent life with an innate tendency to go out and explore the cosmos. Perhaps an inner instinct to return to our original past abode wherever that might have been. Just like the salmon fish instinctively returns to where it was born."

"Daniel, enough of your hypotheses and dreamland fantasies. Let's stick to Mars, we are about to land." Sam interrupted.

They were a few feet from the surface, could see no structures or any sign of activity anywhere. The shuttle kept descending, they realised it was sinking into a pit. It was dark. Only when the roof top shut and the shuttle rested, the entire area lit. It was not large, on the far end a vehicle was parked.

"We have reached, but have to wait a while for the air to stabilize." Ashtok said.

Shortly after, a door opened from a wall and several people emerged, milled around, some headed towards them.

"Who are those people?" Sam asked.

"They are from our planet Urna. Now get ready to disembark." Ashtok said.

The parked vehicle with a streamlined brassy body-shine, transparent roof top and blinking yellow lights around its middle drove up to the shuttle, Ashtok and Ayond were the first to disembark followed by the rest.

David walked away a little distance and asked, "What is behind that wall?"

"One of the many workshops, where we have machinery to acclimatise the planet, someday we will return and show it to you, right now we will stick to our schedule to what we have come for." Ashtok said and entered the vehicle. When all were seated, there was a soft siren and lights on the opposite wall began to blink. All the personnel outside left the premises and exited by the door they had come in.

On the opposite wall a door with blinking lights slid open and the vehicle entered a tunnel, moving at a medium pace for a short while and then picked up speed. It was dark, but the headlights flooded the approaching blackness showing running glimpses of the shape and structure they were meandering through. On two occasions bright light flashed from above through vents. Ayond explained, "That was sun light, there are some areas above where the ground is eroded by wind and natural elements. However, the tunnel is safe, its roof is encased with a special fiber similar to plastic which can stand strong winds and shifting debris. Our only fear is that it might be spotted by earth's probes or even discovered by visiting astronauts."

"Did the Martians build it?" Jim asked.

"No, we did, many years ago, rebuilt their degenerating infrastructure and underground living complexes. One of which you will be visiting shortly." Ayond explained.

"I wonder what type of creatures the Martians look like. Are they friendly?" Jim casually remarked.

"Please do not refer to them as creatures, you have not met them and have already formed an opinion. They might consider you as one. They are good beings, please address and treat them with respect," Ayond advised politely.

The vehicle began to slow down, flashes of yellow and red light began to fill the tunnel and when it came to a halt the lights faded.

They got off onto a platform, from a doorway could see five figures approaching. Ashtok and Ayond moved forward to meet them.

Ayond addressed them in a language that sounded like squeals and squeaks. She held Ashtok by the hand, spoke in English, "This is our Supreme High in person, you had met him in another form when you visited Urna, a stationary cube, but now he is a person like you and I. He is to be addressed as Ashtok." The welcoming party just moved their appendages as a form of greeting. She then introduced the rest, "Meet the Martian gentlemen, they are the highest authority here and to be addressed as the Elders. With the same movements they were greeted.

The team baffled, just stared at their form, biologically ant like in physical structure.

The Elders led them to an elevator, Ayond softly explained to her colleagues that they were several hundred feet below the surface. Minutes later they emerged into a large open area with some of the Martians milling around. Ayond pointed towards a towering wall, "See those windows up there that is where they live, it goes deep into the crust, fully furnished apartments. There are several such living complexes where water is available, like this lake at the far end," pointing to it.

After a brief tour their hosts led them into the towering wall. An elevator took them up to the highest point. They walked through a long corridor and stopped at a window. The view was like looking down from a skyscraper, could see the open area and the lake where they were minutes ago.

David just kept repeating, "Incredible, incredible, couldn't have imagined I am walking with Martians, and to be in this out of the world place. What other wonders are in store for us."

After they had their fill of sightseeing, followed their hosts and entered a large room. Subdued lights, sufficient to see some artifacts on each corner and some paintings on the wall. Two large rectangular tables with chairs were placed opposite each other. On them were tall cylindrical shaped glasses filled to the brim with a greenish liquid. On the opposite table where the Elders sat, the glasses had long straws in them.

Ashtok, and Ayond sat in the middle flanked by the rest. Sitting across were the extra-terrestrials who neither looked human or any other lifeform they could have imagined.

Jim whispered to David sitting next to him, "They look like overgrown ants."

David whispered back, "Be quiet. This is not the time." But Jim began to study and analyse the biological lifeforms sitting across him. "Their bodily form is unique, four arms almost human like in structure, with elbows, wrist, palm with three fingers and a thumb. The rest of their body is very much like ants but with some flesh around the waist. Their tight fit suits covered them entirely and from the size of their shoes, I would say, about one foot long. Their head is complex, the eyes large and rounded. Strangely they are not wearing masks."

Jim's thoughts were interrupted when the Elder sitting in the centre began. "Ashtok, the noble senior and master of planet Urna, before we begin, please enjoy our special nectar to foster the bond between us. Ashtok you are excused from drinking, just touch the glass as a token of your acceptance." All in silence, the Elders began sipping through the straws and the rest picked theirs and relished the drink.

"Wow! That was delicious, what is it made of?" Sam could not resist exclaiming.

"When we meet the next time, we will tell you all about this special fruit." One of the Elders replied him and continued, "Once again, we wish to thank the great one, the Supreme High to visit us in person and wish to extend our gratitude to your people, without their gracious help our civilisation would have been striving for survival or would have even perished. It was your Guardian who found us thousands of years ago and with your generous guidance helped to build our habitats with all the modern conveniences. Also grateful to Ayond who visits us regularly, the teachers she provided are a great help. Over the years they educated us to be like your people. They taught us your language and that of the Earth, we hold them in high esteem.

"You made our world habitable. Long ago, you thought of relocating us on Earth and sent a few as an experiment to adapt to the climatic condition. Your sympathetic intentions were good. Homes suitable to our type of living were carved into hill sides in what is now Turkey and in the Grand Canyon in America. Good thing it failed, because in the long run humans would have hunted them like some kind of animals. We are happy where we are now, except for the water creatures who are a constant threat to our lives. You mentioned once that you will reallocate them elsewhere. This should be your priority before you embark on building cities on the surface, and please as a cautionary advice, with due respect to your friends sitting beside you, don't bring humans here as you are planning. They would bring with them archaic ways of life and weapons of destruction. We have lived in peace and understand the value of harmonious living. That's why we have survived the natural catastrophes that wiped out other lifeforms on our planet. We are confident, your magnanimous work will bring our dead world to life.

"With the climatic change we may find it difficult to adjust, but we are survivors in all adversities. Our little cousins on Earth have survived several extinctions. Our kind are tuned to acclimatise and adjust to changes. Ashtok, you are our noble senior and consider you as the master of our world too, once again thank you for visiting us." The senior Elder concluded.

Ashtok turned his head to right and left, "My human friends have you heard what the Elder had to say about your kind. Your reputation has preceded you here and perhaps elsewhere in the universe. It is not a pleasant gesture. Your specie cannot live in peace on their own world yet dare to exploit space where they are not welcomed. All humans are not bad, there will be some who deserve to be part of us."

Then he turned to the Elder, "Thank you for you noble advice, I shall keep in mind what is best for this world. The water creatures will be dealt with soon, your people will be free from that threat. As for the people we select to bring here will be as good as these sitting with us. Many years ago I embarked on waking this world from its long slumber, I can assure you it will once again blossom as it once did."

The Elders raised their hands above their heads in a gesture of appreciation.

"Thank you," Ashtok said. After a pause he added. "A day will come when there will be children of different species running around playing games and making noises all over as one happy family. They would not be differentiated from being human, Jinn, or of your kind, all will be Martians. That is what I have to say, think about it."

"Before we end this session," one of Elders said looking at the human guests, perhaps to indicate that he had heard the remark Jim had made earlier about them being overgrown ants. "Our race has an ability, as your little ants back home, the gift of telepathic communication. Please feel free to ask any questions.

Jim put up his hand, "You do resemble our little ants, how did you evolve?"

"Nature plays its role in nurturing all forms of life appurtenant to the environment. Take the example of your evolution, nature played its part in making you walk upright to search for food. It took a long time to bring you to what you are today. Same with us and other lifeforms which are now extinct. Due to the environmental inconsistency, breathing the toxic air and food resources available at the time, we adapted to those conditions perhaps nature played a role in reshaping us to adjust to those changes. It did not happen overnight, it took millions of years in the making. Just like some of your species adapting to the catastrophic upheavals, not once but several times. The trick is to find a way how to survive."

David shuffled in his seat and asked. "Soon Mars will have a breathable atmosphere more or less like Earth, how will it affect your survival?"

"Thousands of years ago we endured breathing the fluctuating outside air, a gradual change over millennium of years, our respiratory system began to adapt to the change, that is how we survived. Since our rehabilitation by Ashtok's people, the air inside our complexes were gradually refined in stages to the present level which you people would be able to breathe after certain applications and will not need those masks you are wearing. When Mars has a breathable atmosphere all will adapt to it and be free of gadgets and devices."

"Do you believe in a higher order who shaped your lives?" Daniel asked.

The Elders looked puzzled and exchanged glances.

"I will put it another way, is there a supernatural being that you look up to for help when required?"

"Yes of course, noble Ashtok and able Ayond, but they are not supernatural."

Ayond interrupted Daniel before he would ask another one, "Daniel leave it at that, they don't comprehend what you are driving at"

Fiona looked at Ayond, "May I ask a simpler question?"

Ayond nodded.

"Excuse me sir, to me you all look the same, how can one differentiate between the genders?"

"Very simple, you may not be able to see the difference, but we can. In fact, there are two females sitting opposite you and I am one of them."

Then the Elder addressed Ashtok, "The human we rescued who calls himself Josh-wa, do you want to take him or leave him with us?"

"I think right now he is better off with you, he must not know of our visit."

"With regard to your work on Mars, what is the present status?" An Elder asked.

"The work is progressing well, needs a little more time and as far as the first dome city, the plans are ready. No construction work on the surface until we are absolutely sure that no Earth probes or astronauts are programmed." Ashtok said.

"Should they visit, please don't send them to us, the one we have is sufficient, he is a good guest." The Elder replied promptly, after a pause he added, "Forgive me for asking, how was it made possible for you to be what you are from your former state?"

"Very simple, the people who made the Guardian and me were comprehensive, they had reached the pinnacle of knowledge, implanted their intelligence into our brain, some have more of it and some less, depending on the functions it is programmed to perform. In my case, they have embedded all their data into me and added a catalyst in my brain to continue to self-generate new information. In other words, they understood the brain's evolutionary process which takes years to develop in living beings, but in a laboratory or as in my case has the ability to intellectually multiply indefinitely. The Guardian has to some extent that skill, by using it, constructed my outer form only, and in it transferred my existing faculty of intelligence.

The Elder was somehow confused, "Impressive to learn about the capabilities of the mind, do Earth humans have it too? I wonder....." He was interrupted by the sound of the alarm, the Elders got up and asked their guest to follow them. Went to a corridor and looked down at the open area beside the lake.

Water creatures darted aimlessly lashing mercilessly with their retractable tongues at their victims, in seconds dismembering and swallowing them. Some grabbed their victims and plunged into the water. The second alarm sounded, lethal to their physique, made them disoriented and helpless, drowsily retreated to the water. On the ground below, dismembered body parts were strewn all over.

"Please Ashtok, must get rid of them, we have no means to protect ourselves."

"It will be my priority, I promise you." He said.

After some formalities they left.

Ayond distressed by the scenes said, "You have been thinking of rehabilitating them on Europa or some other moon, it is high time to get rid of them."

They got into the shuttle and soon were back on *The Gentle Stream*. Hours into the flight Ashtok announced, "Seeing those horrid scenes we just witnessed, I have decided to act immediately to go and explore Europa's waters. Be prepared for another venture." Well into the flight, he announced to look at the screen. "See that massive asteroid heading our way, I will send it far away not to cause any harm."

The screen showed a faint object, the reflected sun light off Jupiter outlined its shape and size, a massive chunk of rock about a mile in length rotating and heading towards them. All eyes were fixed to the screen waiting for a zap to disintegrate it, instead its rotation slowed and it began to pulsate left and right as if an invisible force was retarding its acceleration to a stop. Suddenly it flung back into the void with an enormous force, like a tin can blown by a strong wind. Ashtok left the controls to the co-pilot and joined the rest.

"What was that, where has it gone?" David was puzzled.

"It is a new type of weapon I have developed. It is a magnetic force, concentrated well on a point, it can do wonders," Ashtok calmly answered.

"What else do you have on this ship?" David asked.

"Many wonders." He paused, follow me I will show one. They descended to a section in the ship and entered a room. "What is that? So long and slim, can't be more than a few feet in width." Someone exclaimed.

"Simple, it is a kind of submarine for deep see diving with a drilling device. It is seventy five feet long and fifteen feet wide, a bit cramped inside, but comfortable and what it can do is unimaginable."

"What will you drill in a sea?" Sam asked pointing at the nozzle.

"Not in the sea but above it, ice, miles thick, on Jupiter's moons, Europa. That is where we are heading now. Below that ice lies a vast ocean which we are to explore before returning home to Urna. The nozzle, you must watch it when its telescopic drills are activated. They will fan out as wide as the sub. You will enjoy the sight when it comes to play."

"I want a window seat," Fiona exclaimed from the back.

"Everyone will have a window seat, the upper deck is made up of a special transparent material just like glass. Now let us go back and relax until we reach our destination."

Ayond was pleased that Ashtok took the decision to act promptly to start the process of finding a home for the Martian water creatures.

CHAPTER 8

The Gentle Stream orbited Europa. An Icey landscape greeted them, its surface disfigured by linear cracks and streaks crisscrossing in albedo features and ridges that may have been the result of broken ice crust and refrozen to form new patterns around the entire sphere. Sonar wave readings were promising, at several points on the surface the ice was thin with water geysers and erupting water plumes. Selection was made to drill near the South Pole where the ice was thin and fragile. In a happy tone Ashtok said, "Ladies and gentlemen, I have found the spot through which we will enter the ocean below."

They got into the submarine and slipped out into the void, descending gently, inside the passengers watched as the icy surface approached. A few hundred feet from their target the submarine began to adjust gently to a vertical position in a nose dive. The chairs within automatically altered their posture during the process.

"Have your last peep of the outside, soon we'll be going under. Those who can, watch through windows the extending rotary blades coming into motion and inch by inch sinking into the ice." He explained.

The outspread blades began to spin like a fan, the submarine descended gently, a few feet above the ice it remained steady for a few minutes, then inched it way down, the high velocity rotating heated blades fanned the surface scattering icy particles in all directions forming a circular pattern for its entry, on contact, it smoothly penetrated and began to sink gently.

"Can't hear a thing." Sam asked.

"The sub is sound proof, beside there is no air outside to carry the sound." Ashtok said.

"How convenient it is to talk to you while at the controls as if sitting with us." Jim said.

"This is one of its wonders." Ashtok responded.

"How sure are you that the environment down there would be suitable for those creatures to thrive?" David asked.

"We had taken samples of the water some time ago and the analysis were satisfactory. It is very saline as that on Mars, that's why we use filtration there. Temperatures vary in different parts of this ocean, perhaps due to vents spewing hot plumes. Let us hope we find it suitable. Our main purpose is to find any flora that the Martian water creatures can survive on and adapt to the environment."

The burrowing into the ice seemed to last forever, with the external lights they could see a wall of ice around them with an occasional rub against the windows. To fill the time of her non-picturesque odyssey, Fiona started a conversation with Ashtok, "Have you given a name to this sub.?"

"No I have not, could not think of an appropriate name, perhaps sooner or later I will think of one."

"I was thinking of Jules Verne's Nautilus it was a highly sophisticated machine for that time, as is your sub in our time."

"Well as you are keen that I give it a name, I thought of one, I will call it *Fiona* after your name. Any objections?"

"It is an honour, Ashtok. Thank you," Fiona said proudly.

Ashtok made an announcement, "Ladies and gentlemen, I have decided to name my submarine, *Fiona,* after the youngest member of Ayond's team, with you all the first living being to have entered this domain."

Shortly after, *Fiona* went through, fell free in a nose dive into the water. It went down several hundred feet and steadily bounced back to the top hitting solid ice. It rocked from side to side, became steady and buoyant after a while it gradually began to adjust to a horizontal position. The chairs adjusted back automatically. The disturbed water obstructed their vision of the outside, when it settled flood lights gave a view of an endless stretch of water with an icy rooftop above.

Ashtok announced, "Shortly we will begin our dive and explore what mysteries lie in these waters. The outside reading tells me that the water colour is slightly murky, translucent, perhaps will be less foggy as we move on, it has oxygen, hydrogen, nitrogen and carbon dioxide. Surprisingly the water temperature is not much lower than the underground water on Mars, perhaps warmer nearer the vents."

Fiona began to move, gently diving deeper and deeper. Little ridges of varied shapes and sizes came to view then disappeared, at one point it almost collided with a protruding rock shaft, but *Fiona* maneuvered away and continued to dive. The dial showed three thousand feet, a happy sight was when they spotted an intermingled cluster of floating vines that hit against the sub and drifted away. An uneven sea floor appeared, at several points broken and dipped into an abyss, shortly after came a flat plain that stretched for miles. The sub slowed to a walking pace, a velvety substance like tall grass was spotted covering a large area, within it materialised the first sign of living organism, a transparent snake like, covered with spikes and fins. Out of the grass a ball or what looked like a clump of sea weeds or urchins sprang to action, unfolded its wrappings and attached itself to the unsuspecting snake, curled back into a clump trapping it. Further on, several feet long spiral vines floated freely and entangled any thing that came in its way. One of those clumps met its doom as it came in its path.

At one point the floor teamed with a variety of weeds, shrubs and tiny marine life, closely resembling shrimps, snail fish, sorceress eel and the like, all close to the hot spouting vents. The topography of the seabed hosted a varied landscape, from ridges to escarpments, open grounds and undulating rolling hills. Vegetation in some parts were dense where marine life thrived. One of the long vines rose vertical and tried to attach itself to the sub, but on contact it slid down and remained motionless.

"Very odd, it just withered away as it touched the sub? Something has immobilized it, what could it be?" Sam said.

"I can make a guess," Ashtok said, "Perhaps it attached itself to a warm part, it just immobilised or sadly killed it. The interesting thing is that there is active marine life. The water temperature is much warmer here, seems to vary from spot to spot. Perhaps due to tidal activity similar to ecosystems around hydrothermal vents on Earth where deep down in oceans there is no sun light and yet life thrive as it is here. The possible answer to this is that in some cases bacterial species do not rely on light, they live by using chemical energy derived from minerals and chemical compounds from vents to convert carbon dioxide into sugar." Ashtok was interrupted when something large darted by, the sub stopped, turned around and located the object, focused its lights on a stationery object about six feet tall.

It was an animal of some sort, had a body shape of a Kangaroo standing upright. On closer look it had two short tentacles as arms and a flat tail on which it rested. The head can roughly be described as a rugby ball resting sideways on its shoulders with several pencil thin hornlike features on either side and one in the middle slightly bigger. No visible eyes, but an elongated mesh like fleshy mantle shade with tiny eyes across the forehead, shaped and resembling that of a giant clamp. A rounded orifice for the mouth. On 'seeing' or feeling the presence of something unusual that disturbed the water, it began to jump side to side. The sub's bright lights were turned slightly away from it. The creature stood firm and facing whatever was in front of it, showing no sign of fear or alarm.

Ashtok was amazed at the sight. "This creature is perhaps the most intelligent down here and a brave one too. I am going out to meet it."

Dressed in his specially tailored aquatic suit Ashtok stepped out. He walked to the Kangaroo shaped figure and stood still a few

73

feet away. Both faced each other and waited. Suddenly the still water between them began to vibrate with ripples like waves close apart in swift successions, moments later it stopped. Ashtok got the message, he reciprocated by copying the gesture, but his waves were further apart and more placid. The creature copied Ashtok's gestures, then a few moments of calm. The creature bent over with his tentacles grabbed sand from the sea floor and threw it randomly at Ashtok. It was reciprocated.

The childish sand throwing game continued for some time. The creature began to move towards Ashtok. It began to feel the form in front of it with its little side tentacles and facial pencil like flanges sizing what it was touching. Moved back and began to spin on it tail in circles, uttering a high frequency pitch very similar to whale calls, and from all around more creatures began to emerge and assemble around them. They were orderly and sat on their tails. To the onlookers within the submarine the sight was awesome.

None of the assembled creatures made any gestures but stood motionless. From the one standing opposite him small faint ripples began to flow towards Ashtok, to the creature's disappointment not receiving a response, it began to utter a low pitch clicking, resembling a Morse code. Ashtok was taken by surprise. It took him moments to bring his mechanical brain to understand the configuration the creature was conversing with. It did not take long for the artificial intelligence to decipher its message. To Ashtok at first it was either expressing submission, or perhaps a form of greeting. However, he decided to copy those clicks, no sooner, the creature began to spin once again on its tail. Perhaps an expression of joy or conceivably both had established a communication medium by which they understood each other.

Resting on its tail, it resumed its clicks with high and low pitches. It took Ashtok a while to finally understand what was being said. The creature was narrating how they had come to be in this place. A tough ordeal when some people like him forcibly removed them from their home which had plenty of food but their captors soon realised the shortage of diet available to them in their new home, promptly they provided them with more food resources brought in from their world. The creature then asked Ashtok to bring his people and live with them.

Ashtok regretfully explained that they come from a different world and cannot survive in a watery world but promised to bring more food and a lifeform that would adapt to those conditions and keep them company. But cautioned against their aggressive nature which needed to be controlled.

The aquatic creature simply communicated that aggression comes when one is hungry and food supply is limited. It explained that the food available is not sufficient for additional beings, and as far as their aggressive nature, nothing to worry about, they know how to handle such situations. Its final words were to provide them with more food.

With those words Ashtok was more than pleased and bend over, scooped the floor with both hands and threw the loam high up. The aquatic creature reciprocated and both parted.

On his return to the *Fiona* all were puzzled at what had gone on outside, Ashtok just sat at the controls and said in a low voice, "What a unique lifeform, it was not easy at first to pick up the form of communication, but simple enough to decipher and converse. The bottom line is whatever shapes and sizes those creatures are, there is a humane aspect in their nature. Perhaps that quality exists in most lifeforms. They are another displaced entity and lonely, will be happy to have new companions. I have achieved what I have come for, at the same time our Martian friends would be glad to get rid of their adversaries.

CHAPTER 9

It was not unusual for Ashtok to sit alone and think or reminisce of gone by epochs in terms of millenniums of years. It began with visualising Mars blooming with life, Martians, humans, Jinn and people of Urna all of different races and species flourishing side by side, comprising a community perhaps unique in the Milky Way Galaxy. "It is my dream to achieve this feat." He said to himself. Then his thoughts went back to the time on his home planet, when his makers depended on his solace and helped them to make the Keepers, the Guardian being one of them who had landed on Urna. The Keepers were to serve the dwindling race which due to sterility caused by natural catastrophe, a unique rainfall triggered the extinction of all living beings and plant life. With no more use for the Keepers, it was a wise decision by him, the master machine as he was then called by his makers, to ask them to go out and seek worlds where they could benefit others with their knowledge. It was the Guardian who had brought the master machine to Urna which became his new home. "Had it not been for the Guardian, I would most probably be rotting in that secluded structure they had housed me in on my planet. I am also indebted to the Guardian for reinventing me from a stationary cube, a master machine, to what I am today, Ashtok a living entity. How I love to be among the living." (x) Ashtok said to himself.

He felt nostalgic and decided to call the Guardian to have a chat and at the same time to appraise him with the situation on Earth.

Ashtok walked to a desk, activated a monitor, minutes later the Guardian appeared in the form of a hologram. The two began to converse in an encrypted language only they could understand.

"It is hopeless," The Guardian began, "On the surface the New World Order is working perfectly but many nations have invented codes and sly methods to communicate and achieve their devious activities, just as before. The evil bug is within their nature, nothing can eradicate it."

"What is your verdict, any hope for improvement or correcting the situation?" Ashtok asked.

"In my opinion, none. I think we should leave them to settle their differences or blow themselves apart. As in many other worlds, civilizations were wiped out through wars, diseases, natural catastrophes and the list goes on, nothing new for the humans. This planet is beautiful and would hate to let it to go to waste. People here have not realized it, they only seek wealth and power."

Ashtok remained silent for several minutes, thinking.

"In the next few months I want you to do the following, write down what I am requesting you to do." Ashtok instructed the Guardian, "Starting from the history of the development of the human race coming up to the age of reason, say from about five thousand BCE to date,

1. Collect as much as you can all books written by prominent authors and their biographies.

2. Prominent and outstanding people who shaped the destinies of their nations and influenced the world.

3. Prominent men and women who contributed to the sciences and technological development.

4. All works of music and the lives of the composers starting from the sixth century of the current era. Same for the works of art and their artists including architects.

5. The good people who propagated the rules of law and order for the promotion of peace and harmony to mankind.

6. History of religion, from 5000 BCE to current days, its growth and influence on social development.

7. I leave any other subject you may feel should be included to this list.

"All to be secured in water tight material and packaging."

The Guardian just nodded his head, though in his mind he had a question to ask, "Why all this?" But dared not question his master.

Ashtok continued alone thinking for many hours.

Impulsively contacted Ayond. "How about collecting your team to spend an afternoon together at you residence, how about the day after."

Ayond being the administrator of the planet, was glad to oblige as it would also give her a break and meet the rest which she had not for some time.

Her team was well settled on Urna, engaged in contributing their skills in various fields; Sam and Aishtra busied themselves in public works, David, Jim and Saeed the Egyptian spent their time in organising the library and museum that housed all the documents and artifacts brought from earth. Soon they would be neck deep in more that would be coming. Daniel and Fiona sat with scholars and elders, enjoyed their anecdotes of long ago and how they shaped the destiny of their social order.

It was a beautiful sunny afternoon on the open terrace at Ayond residence. Under the shade of the gigantic tree which spread its branches well over the entire area. At one side chairs were arranged with a long table in the middle, opposite at far end beside the trunk of the tree was a chair and a coffee table.

The guests arrived and took their seats, informally conversed and nibbled at what was in front of them. Shortly after, Ashtok entered and with a wave of his hand greeted all. Ayond escorted him to the chair beside the trunk of the tree. He was pleased to see on the table a plates with tea shoots and another had tea leaves. He said to her before sitting down, "To be honest I was missing this stuff, one of the reasons for the meeting, the aroma from those shoots is always in my mind," He looked up and addressed the others, "Forgive me, even I have a weakness. Let's enjoy what we have before us and then get to business."

He went through the ritual of sniffing and chewing, when all done, he raised his head to the gapping on lookers and uttered, "That was great Ayond, I must have a garden of my own someday."

Ayond just looked at him and thought, "That will be the day when a supreme machine can achieve that feat, let him fantasise." Her thought were interrupted when Ashtok began.

"Ladies and gentlemen, I feel so different when I am with you, we have established a bond that any action I wish to take concerning your home planet must have your concurrence. I belong to Urna but because of you and in my present status as a being, I have become more indebted for the help we received from you during the last years spent on your world and makes me obliged to have your views, after all it was your Garden of Eden.

"The Guardian has reported that a spaceship more sophisticated than the previous ones has left for Mars with four astronauts and is due to land in a few months' time. This would be their third attempt. The first one met with the demise of two astronauts and the third, the only survivor, is the guest of the Martians, the people who look like ants in your terminology. The second mission left after spending about two weeks, found nothing of importance. Now we are expecting their third attempt. On Mars we are deeply involved in the climatic structural processes, though their landing area will most likely be at the location where their previous missions landed, away from our activities, yet can't take any chances of them accidentally seeing what we are doing. We have to send them back as soon as they land. Gently we will tell them to leave and with a bit of humorous note to ease their exit."

David got up, "Ashtok, that is unkind, can't they spend a while."

"No, for the good of our work, sometimes we have to be cruel. In the long run humans would benefit from what we are doing. It is too early for them to know."

He then explained the way the astronauts to be received and sent back. The plan sounded like scenes from a comic book and The Twilight Zone movies. "Ayond will be in charge of the rehearsals." He added.

"I have a request to make. We keep referring to the residents of this planet as ant like, it is not appropriate, can't we think of a name more suitable, after all they are the Martians." David said demandingly.

"Very thoughtful David, I leave it to you all to come out with one."

Days before the Mars – 3 Mission was due, Ashtok, Ayond and her colleagues left for Mars and waited in *The Gentle Steam* in its invisible form. Mars – 3 arrived, the ship was left orbiting and the four astronauts descended in a shuttle and landed near the Habitat of previous missions. An astronaut emerged laboriously carrying a camera with a tripod. He placed it a few feet away facing the shuttle. The second also carried a camera placed it further away facing the other way, to the open terrain. The other two joined them. All four stood in front of the first camera, waved their hands for the millions watching on their television sets back home. They bent over and with their gloved hands touch the soil scooped a handful and threw the grit into the air, some of which landed on their headgear. The captain stretched both arm up and cried out loudly, "We are here Mars, show yourself, hide no secrets from us!" They all joined hands and danced in a circle. All that activity was being watched. "Let them have a little more time then we go and join their merry making. "Ashtok said.

The astronauts moved a little further away from the shuttle in front of the second camera and planted a flag, not of any country but was white with two hemispheres in colour, one showing Asia, Europe, Africa and Australia with a portion of Antarctica. The other half had north and South America with the remaining part of Antarctica. Around the top half of the flag, it said, *'The People of Earth'*. A brief prayer was offered. They picked partners and danced. All that activity was recorded by the second camera. Their joy was soon cut short, they froze where they stood, petrified.

Approaching from a distance, almost like a mirage, as they got closer they could see human forms walking merrily holding hands led by a taller figure.

The Captain nervously moved and unknowingly blocked the camera's view. He said, "What the hell is that? Look human, not wearing any suites and their faces are covered with some sort of a mask. Perhaps they are Martians, let me do the talking," Bravely but tensely, he stepped a few feet and raised a hand in greetings. His back was still blocking the camera. There was no reciprocal gesture from the approaching squad as it continued to advance.

They stopped ten feet away from him, the taller person came up to the captain. Dwarfed by the towering figure of Ashtok, seeing the colour of his skin and not wearing a mask, the captain was at a loss to utter a single word.

Ashtok with a heavy masculine voice spoke, "I am sure you all can hear me, I am talking through the same frequency you communicate with each other. If you can hear me raise your hands." They obediently did.

"Welcome Earth people, I am sure you have enjoyed your brief stay here, sorry but you have to leave, please pack up your equipment and depart. As a befitting send-off, my friends here would like to have some fun with you." He turned and with the wave of his hand, Ayond and her colleagues darted at the astronauts, squealing and yelping they rushed and hugged the dumbfounded astronauts who stood bewildered and could not decide how to react. Held their hands and forcibly drawn to dance, exchanged partners and swirled, during their romp and commotion the camera tripod was hit and fell.

The astronauts in their heavy suits were like pillars, helplessly aghast as they were being passed from one person to the other like a claret jug.

Ashtok watched the display as programmed to ease the astronauts' exit. Seeing the miserable state the astronauts were going through and fearing anyone of them falling and damaging his or her space suite, with a loud voice he asked them to stop. "Enough of our welcoming reception, let the unwanted visitors pack up and leave." He turned to the astronauts, "Tell those who sent you not to attempt to come again, this is a firm warning. Have a pleasant journey."

The captain fretfully moved close to Ashtok, "You raise your hand if you can hear me?"

Ashtok raised a hand.

"This is crazy, who are you guys, and you speak English too. None of you wear any suits only those hideous masks and behave like school children" The captain said with a quivering commanding voice.

"Don't get closer Jim, these people are crazy, perhaps they are starving for company." One of the female astronauts warned from a distance.

"I am not afraid of them nor the big hulk who is dressed differently and wears no suit or mask. Who is he to tell us what to do?" The captain said, then looked at Ashtok, "Whoever you are and the freaks you are with, stop this madness and let us get on with what we have come for. Only then we will leave." He retorted.

Ashtok, didn't appreciate the word hulk, so he decided to have some fun. Using his ability to turn into light waves, his body began to light up with a strong blue haze, as a bright beam shot out upwards and settled on their shuttle. The astronauts, stunned, amazed and speechless stood with their mouths wide open. They all simultaneously uttered, "Ohhhh," fear had taken hold of them.

Ashtok took a dive and landed next to the captain. "Did you see what this hulk can do? I can vaporise your shuttle with one breath. Do you want me to show you?"

The captain got the message, he was dealing with a power more than what he could handle. Submissively he said in a trembling voice, "No sir and sorry I did not mean to offend you. What are you, this planet is dead you can't be a Martian?"

Ashtok politely said, "I cannot give you an answer, be good enough and all of you get into your shuttle, go to your ship and leave for home."

Obediently and sullenly they collected their equipment and began boarding. The captain said, I am leaving the Earth flag to remind you of us. Keep it safe."

"Will do, and don't forget to tell your bosses not to attempt another visit, they may not get a better. Have a pleasant journey and good bye."

Ashtok and his team waved pleasantly as the shuttle lifted off. The astronauts did not reciprocate, kept swearing inaudible curses, the captain joined in, "Let's get the hell out of here before he zaps us. That giant of a man or creature, whatever he is, was most obnoxious, unruly and uncivil, didn't have the courtesy to let us spend even a day," the captain said crossly.

"And did you see the display of his powers, turning into light and darting around. He is some kind of Superman." One of the females commented.

The other girl added, "A Martian Superman, and if those other nutty guys have such powers, I am sorry to say that this planet is one big mad house."

"You both are as nutty to think of Martians and Superman." The captain stopped and pondered, "Come to think of it, that was a superhuman form, the rest were living beings." He paused, "What am I talking about, I am getting nutty as you both. Perhaps we did experience a mirage of some sort and hallucinated and like idiots gave in to our whims. How stupid we were, Mars is dead."

"Sorry Jim, I disagree with you, four of us could not have hallucinated and it was not a mirage, the whole thing was real. We felt their touch us and the way they danced was marvelous." One of the females said then tunefully she began to sing, "I could have danced all night...."

"Shut up Jane, get me a cup of coffee, I have to think how we are going to convince the bosses when we return. I said a cup of coffee please." The captain said hotly.

The other female astronaut reminiscent, "Remember that movie, The Martian Chronical where the astronauts hallucinated seeing their loved ones...." Jim banged his fist on the table and rested his head on the palm of his hands, "I can't think anymore, must have my coffee." Then whispered to himself, "Did we really see those freaks."

"Yes sir we did," The male astronaut put in lightly, "And we were booted out, perhaps we needed a visa."

Back on Mars Ashtok said, "Sorry for them but it had to be done for the betterment of our cause and theirs too. At present we cannot take any chances and be exposed to an inquisitive race who can't live in harmony on their world and want to explore new ones."

They got back into *The Gentle Stream*, Ashtok made an announcement. "As we are on Mars, let me show you one of our workshop facility to give you an idea of what we have been doing for many years."

The ship flew a short distance and landed, they got into a shuttle, hovered over a barren spot, the ground opened and they descended into a pit. After the formalities to disembark were completed they walked to a wall, a small door slid open and they entered. A vehicle drove them into a colossal underground cavity. They got off and entered a large workshop, inside was a grotesque looking machine humming endlessly, from it tubes like tentacles rose up to the ceiling.

"This machine we call *The Oxygenator*, loosely translated from our language, beside what the name indicates it also stabilises other gases required to have a breathable atmosphere. We have put many of them all over the planet and all are doing well. Hopefully very soon we will achieve a suitable atmosphere. In the beginning a simpler facial mask will be required until the air is fully refined. Within the planned domed cities masks will not be worn as they will be fully conditioned with controlled environment. But for now and until such time, have to bear the inconvenience of wearing them on the outside.

"What we are doing here is very complex for you to understand, for many centuries we are at it, kept on improving the equipment. The signs we are getting are satisfactory, showing the required changes. The fundamentals are already woven to produce a weather to trigger the elements. It can happen any day."

For the visitors it was an educational tour and understood the extent of hard work put in to achieve a dramatic change to the planet's atmosphere.

Meanwhile, the four astronauts settled on their journey back home. The captain recapped their experience, how to narrate their story to the bosses on arrival. "Those were real people, definitely human, except that obnoxious bully. There is no life on Mars, perhaps they were the survivors of a secretly sent assignment by one of the space pioneer countries on an experimental suicide mission with no chance of returning back, luckily met some kind of life and are living happily."

"What about that giant of a man with uncanny powers. He could not be human or man- made, besides neither our Space Agency nor any other country had the capability to send astronauts beyond the moon. It is out of the question to assume that assumption."

"Jane has a point, if we rule out humans, then there must be some kind of life on Mars."

"If there is, our probes would have spotted them." The other astronaut put in.

"Two of our probes were lost out there sometime back, perhaps knocked down by the Martians." Jim said calmly.

"Let us not theorise and worry our heads solving a sixty million dollar question, we will leave it to the brains at the Agency. For now, let us think how we are going to tell our story. Nobody will believe us and brand us as space lunatics. We are going to maintain radio silence until we are a couple of days before arrival." The captain said and added, "That monster of a hulk, how am I going to explain him to them."

"Just tell them he was a superman," Jane put in.

Jim was not amused, "We have to tell our story as it happened, it is up to them to believe it or not."

Their journey back was uneventful, four humans encased in a tube shaped spaceship, divided into sections with all the amenities, claustrophobic and monotonous, yet they endured passing time nonchalantly. Their months of seclusion were coming to an end.

A million miles from home, Jim called the Space Agency, "This is Mars-3, calling Space Agency." There was no response for a long time. He kept repeating, finally a voice answered, "Did you say Mars-3, is that you Jim?"

"Yes, it is me, we are coming in, we'll explain our silence, and all of us are in good shape."

"We lost contact a few hours after your landing, we kept trying for many days, finally gave up thought you had a major problem or something went wrong with your communication equipment. Mars – 4 is being prepared for your rescue."

"Had no major problem or communication failure, we were booted out, can't tell you more, will explain when we meet."

"When you landed your recordings were terrific, especially planting the flag and the dancing bit, the camera must have been knocked out as later we could only see the sky. After that all went blank. You are back earlier than scheduled." The man from the Agency said.

"It is a long story, you will hear it when we come in, will contact again before entry."

Their arrival was momentous. The director of the Space Agency and heads of departments were there to receive the crew of Mars -3.

The ship landed on a bright sunny day in California on a runway different from their predecessors who on entry parachuted down on to an ocean. They were greeted by a shower of flowers as they emerged from the ship. They were driven to a quarantine room for a medical checkup. The procedures were easy and after four days were cleared to be met only by three senior officials of the Agency.

The director shook hands "Jim we are glad you are all well and have accomplished an incomplete mission. Forgive the sarcasm, what made you short cut your stay. You said something like being booted out. By whom, the Martians?" He said jokingly with a cynical smile looking back at his companions.

"How did you guess?" Jim replied looking squarely at him.

"You are not serious, jokes aside tell us what really happened to make made you abort the mission?"

"Why don't you all sit down, I will tell you the whole story whether you believe it or not. I have three astronauts who were with me who have witnessed it all."

Obediently they sat down, Jim asked his colleagues to sit beside him, looking at the Space Agency seniors drawing their full attention, he began.

"Gentlemen, please keep an open mind. What I am about to tell you may sound ludicrous. We are not alone, there is life out there on that dead planet we call Mars."

Jim waited and looked at the placid expressions on the three faces in front of him. "Go on." One of them said softly.

"They materialised out of nowhere and greeted us with actions like some crazy freaks, their leader was much taller and bigger than the rest with shiny golden brown skin, an obnoxious hulk who could turn himself into a beam of light. There were men and women, swarmed on us, hugged, kissed and forced us to dance. Later their leader the hulk, threatened us to leave or else. Obviously under those circumstances we had no choice. No way out, he could have eliminated us with one zap of his deadly rays."

"Do you mean to tell us that you all really met Martians, or let me put it in another way, met people up there and their leader was some kind of super being with obnoxious manners?

"That was exactly what we had experienced."

The three senior Space Agency personals exchanged a few words with each other, the director got up and walked to the astronauts. Studied their facial expressions, they were grim and sullen. The director remembered a message on a probe which was redirected back some years ago with a warning to keep away from Mars. Inwardly he did not reject their story but had to find a reasonable way out to put them at ease.

Jim suddenly remembered the camera, "Scenes of our arrival and the fiasco, some of it at least, why didn't I think of it? I am sure there must be some footage of our senseless dancing with that lot."

"We have seen your transmission, nothing extraordinary."

"No harm in viewing those scenes again, I am sure something may turn up." Jim said.

The camera was brought. Scenes of the four touching the Martian soil, playing with the grit and the planting of the flag. The hazy mirage like apparition was overlooked by the Agency personal when they watched the transmission sent from Mars. "You may have missed that part." The captain said.

"The only thing we saw was empty terrain and then someone came in front of the camera and blocked the view." The Agency Director said.

"Let me play it again, please concentrate." The captain ran the tape over and over again. On scrutiny they could glimpse the foggy figures of human forms for a split second when the captain unknowingly moved in front of the camera blocking the view. A little later a hand going around his waist, moving and swirling as in a dance. All the time showing his back, another astronaut came close and bumped into him, both moved back hitting the camera knocking it down and pointing to the sky, but the sound of commotion and vocal excited utterances were clearly audible on the sound track.

The Agency men moved to one side, talked briefly and came to the astronauts, the director said, "We will study the tapes further, meanwhile you will have to stay in quarantine as routine formality for a month in a special home. Your families can come and meet you under strict supervision, but no talk about Martians or your trip." In principle the Agency men believed in their encounter but decided not to divulge it to anyone for fear of publicity. They decided to keep it strictly to themselves.

On their own, the three senior Space Agency men watched the tape over and over several times in a strictly closed room. The director said, "The mirage like apparition is of real beings, and that person they are referring to as an obnoxious hulk who turned to a beam of light must be someone like the Guardian who is running the New World Order, there must be many of them. Though they come from a different planet called Urna, the chances are they have a presence on Mars."

"Why not ask the Guardian, if they are involved, which I am sure they are, he can get us clearance for future missions." One of the Agency men suggested.

"No Richard, it won't work. We were explicitly warned to keep away by a message put in our probe which we had sent to Mars and it was redirected back. I am sure they are up to something and don't want us there. Better to stay away for some time. The Guardian must be watching every move we make and reporting to his boss. Sending astronauts would be risky, lucky the Mars – 3 guys came back alive." The director said to his colleagues.

"Somehow we have to find out what is going on out there. Perhaps send a probe to Pluto, on its way to peep onto Mars and their planet Urna.

"Forget it Richards, they are smarter than you think. Not worth the risk."

CHAPTER 10

The Guardian was in conversation with Ashtok, "A new situation had risen, a Middle Eastern head of state was assassinated in a night club while on vacation to a small neighbouring country. The hot headed public demanded the government to punish them to avenge the murder of their leader. Without warning they attacked the smaller weak nation. Some countries in the region took sides and the war escalated without any hope of coming to a stop. The super powers and the New World Order have failed in their peace efforts."

Ashtok promptly replied, "Waste no time, an exemplary action must be shown to the world as to what happens to those who take matters in their own hands. Eliminate the aggressor nation, take over their entire weaponry and military installations then report to me."

The Guardian wasted no time, sent one of the small crafts. It hovered on the capital city displaying its presence, starting from the outskirts it began a circular approach letting loose continuous fiery discharges stopping at its centre. In a short while the remains below were heaps of rubble and smouldering ashes.

The Guardian made an announcement to the world, "I have punished the one who initiated the war and give a warning to those who participated, if repeated the punishment will be more severe to the aggressor and those who take sides." He was brief. Order was restored in the region and was reported to Ashtok, "The situation is under control, we will have some peace at least for some time. Knowing human psyche, this is not the end of their manipulation."

Few months after the assault on the aggressor Middle Eastern nation, a commercial organization bought an abandoned ruin of a large complex which was a secret headquarters of military operations in the late twentieth century, located somewhere in a forest in the heart of Europe. Most of its structure still stood but in depleted condition. Renovations included a ten feet high wire fence and an electronic alarm system, sensitive to the touch and surveillance cameras randomly placed on a number of trees, discretely camouflaged to blend with the environment to send the image of an intruder. At night bright lights from different angles flooded the entire outer surroundings.

The proprietors of this facility called themselves The Avenger, a clandestine organization set up by seven multi-billionaires from different countries, their staff comprised of notorious criminals who supervised the premises inside and out day and night. Their aim was to disrupt the New World Order and assassinate the top personnel that ran it, mainly its head; the Guardian. They knew his unlimited abilities and being non-human. To get rid of him would collapse the Order. The head of the organization was addressed as the Master. By their own right the proprietors were well-known respectable figures in the financial and business world. All of them enjoyed that reputation. No one would ever suspect them of their heinous selfish motives.

In his inaugural address to his partners, the Master began, "We are all set, in this complex no will guess what goes on inside, the authorities know our reputations and some of us being royalty they understand our security requirements, they will not bother us. Let me appraise you with the good news. I have found a source to obtain the latest type of explosive devises or bombs, they are so small, can fit in a pocket and each can bring down a block. Another feature, they are camouflaged by a chemical, can't be detected by any known means and can be set to detonate automatically if anyone tries to fiddle with them. At the same time we shall install CCTV to supervise and electronically activated them from here. I will have a keyboard, each button is marked with a number, a chart will give the location of each bombs and on a screen will have a visual. Pressing a button on the keyboard can activate any bomb. In those countries where they will be placed, the authorities will be warned, anyone that tries to find them, we will detonate and cause the death of many. The touch of one finger, can cause damage the world has not seen. No one can get smart with us, we are well secured.

"We can have an unlimited supply as long as we can manage the cost. It will be in millions of dollars, and the commission fee to the procurers who are two government officials is twenty million. All of you are heads of rich nations and billionaire businessmen, can easily fund this project. It is worth the investment, some of you come from that vanquished nation like me. Our cousin, the head of our nation was brutally murdered and we were punished instead of that nation in which the crime was committed. What kind of justice is that and all due to its head, the one who calls himself the Guardian. We want revenge, at the same time take control of the world and do away with the so called New World Order.

"We have the means and infrastructure to rule. The super powers will be made impotent after planting those devises at strategic location in their capitals. In this building we will have control on each and every bomb, anyone who tries to be clever, just press a button and *boooomb* it goes. A few *boooombs* will set the world at our feet. The cost is high but in the long run we will benefit many folds. I have sent feelers to some rich friendly nations through very confidential sources, and the feedback is encouraging. They doubt its success but are committed to contribute to our cause. My contacts have also warned them that if they ever double cross our agreement in any way they would pay a heavy price by the same bombs they are paying for."

"How can you infiltrate into those strategic areas like the headquarters of the New World Order, well secured, a fly cannot get in." One of the members asked.

"With the dollar you can move mountains." The Master began, "Let me explain my fool proof plan, I have arranged for a hundred briefcases of the same colour and size and fill them with some innocent publicity material for an attractive low fare cruise during the coming holidays. Of course it is a fictitious offer, made to appear genuine, goodwill for the Christmas and New Year season. Some of them will carry the bombs for planting at strategic locations in North America. Our first target is the New World Order building in New York with all its staff and of course its head, the Guardian. Two bombs will be placed for double insurance, one under his chair and another in the building. This will be done before the closing session of the Order before Christmas. Delivery to European locations is not as difficult.

"Transporting the bombs to the United States is not going to be easy, but nothing is impossible. I have figured it out. An executive jet with a pilot and three females, its destination will be the State of Ohio. My contact there has found the perfect spot, an open farm area, he has given me the coordinates and it looks perfect. Before reaching that spot, the pilot will call the tower and report engine trouble, show panic as if the aircraft is out of control. The pilot and the three females with the briefcases containing the publicity material and the bombs will parachute off the plane near the spot where our men would be waiting. By the time the plane crashes and the authorities are distracted, the four will be driven off the area by our men on the ground and merge with the public. The rest is easy, in New York they will stay in an apartment. There they will remove all the bombs from all the briefcases and store them away, then place two in one meant for the New World Order building."

"Excuse me Master, you said the bombs can detonate if fiddled with, don't you think such a thing may happen while jumping off the plane?" One of the members asked.

"The bombs are not activated. They will be set by our men prior to planting them. Only then will detonate if tempered with and electronically by me pressing a button on the key board. Of course they are all treated with the camouflage chemical. The two for the New World Order building will not be set to detonate by any movement, only by me to have that pleasure. To continue with what I was saying. The trick is how to deliver the two bombs to the New World Order building. Five hundred feet in all directions are heavily guarded and monitored. It is impossible for anyone to walk in without clearance. We will have two small vans packed with the briefcases carrying innocent publicity material, remember the bombs were removed, each van will carry fifty, the delivery to them would be forty cases and the balance ten in each vehicle are for some other client, of course a fictitious one to throw away any suspicions. In the second van one of the cases will have the two bombs treated with the anti-detection chemicals and are not activated, hidden away under the floor. The first van would be inspected at the main gate and pass. The second, having the same publicity material would be a routine check. Once cleared they would be accompanied by security guards to the delivery area inside the premises. Both vans would be driven and assisted by gorgeous looking females. In the second van the driver's charming conversation will keep the security guard distracted, while inside the vehicle one of the girls will retrieve the case with the bombs from under the floor and place it with the rest. During unloading, the girls will assist in handing over the cases to the publicity department staff, one they know and who is on our pay role, would be handed over the special case with the bombs."

"Master, forgive me for interrupting," One of the accomplices asked. "What if the security guard decides to sit with girl inside the second van, she will not be able to retrieve the hidden case, and my second question is, the person working in the building, how can we trust him?"

"The van is small in size, sufficient space for a slim girl to fit in with all the cases. The security man has to sit with the driver, as far as your second query, yes we have a person who is related to one of our men, young, ambitious and can be trusted. Somehow through his sly skills managed to get employed there. We paid him fifty thousand dollars in advance and another fifty after the job is done. His job is to place the bombs securely, one under the Guardian's chair and the other anywhere in the assembly building."

Someone else asked, "Master, how will our man plant the bombs with all the security?"

"After the security inspection of the assembly hall, our man who is an employee there will walk in casually with couple of cases in hand minutes before the start of the session and place the cruise publicity material in font of each member, at the same time will place a bomb under the chair of the Guardian. Should there be another security check after that, the bomb will not show as it is camouflaged and can do no harm even if the chair is moved. The second bomb will be placed elsewhere in the building."

"If I may ask about the fate of our friends and relatives head of states. They all will be killed."

The Master with an air of confidence spoke, "None will be attending and they will be represented by their ambassadors. Sad to see them go, sacrificed for a noble cause. When that building blows up, a few other explosions will take place in some capitals. What else can be better?" He concluded and lit a cigar. After a heavy drag he let out a cloud of smoke and added, "We will then announce to the world that we are in control. Who in their right minds would oppose or move a finger against us." After a few more drags at his cigar he added, "Waiting anxiously for the day and the moment I shall press the button to exterminate the Guardian and his cronies. You all will be here to witness it."

CHAPTER 11

One afternoon Ashtok sat with Ayond and talked about the positive reports he was receiving from the main weather control centre on Mars. Happily he added, "I deserve a holiday, am thinking of a brief visit to Earth. How about joining me, see the monuments we had erected during our long stay there, I was a stationary cube then, the Guardian kept me posted with what was done, much before you were born. Such a trip would be refreshing for both of us. At the same time will take the opportunity to witness the Christmas and New Year festivities with the Guardian after the closing session of the New World Order."

"How lucky you and Guardian to have lived that long to boast about your longevity."

"As I have always said, there advantages and disadvantages for being what we are."

"I suggest we plan to reach a day after the closing session of the New World Order. If we arrive earlier the Guardian would be distracted by our presence."

"This is the only time we can travel, I have plenty scheduled to do on Mars. I promise you, we will make ourselves scarce and he would not know. Finish with our tour of North and South

America, after the Guardian gets free will contact him and enjoy the festivities then visit the east and the tea growing areas."

"Agreed," Ayond said.

During their journey to Earth, Ayond enjoyed the luxurious comforts of *The Gentle Stream*. Ashtok spent most of his time watching documentaries and silent movies.

As they passed the asteroid belt between Jupiter and Mars, Ashtok said, "Do you know that all these rocks once were part of a thriving world. I have studied thousands of fragments and surprisingly found traces of lifeforms and some metallic remains of objects. Some asteroids were of a different composition from the rest, they were quite similar to some of the moons of Jupiter. Which only means one thing, that world must have had an unhappy ending, a stray planetoid must have plunged into it, reducing it to what you see today. The intruder did not escape unpunished. After the catastrophic impact, the gravitational pull of Jupiter sent it spinning like a drunken fool, breaking it into fragments that formed some of the Galilean moons. Mars too did not escape entirely, heavy electrical discharges and atmospheric anomalies caused the extinction of life, with the exception of the Martian Ants who managed to survive. Two large chunks of rocks from that disaster got caught by Mars to form its moons, Phobos and Deimos."

All that was new to Ayond.

"Speaking about the Martian Ant species, I thought of a name, if you approve we will start addressing them as such. They would also be happy to have a proper name." Ayond said.

"What is it?"

"Marants, a combination of the words Mar for Mars and ants."

"Sound very appropriate, so let it be, inform all concerned."

Their journey was enlightening and refreshing. They landed on an open field a few miles northwest of New York, away from any human activity.

"The ship is in its invisible form, hard luck for anyone bumping into it. Being in a solitary open area only stray cattle or birds might bang their heads." Ashtok commented casually.

The next day they took off, visited Central America, the Peruvian and Bolivian sites of antiquity in South America. "We were here much before you were born, you may have read our files." After extensive sightseeing excursions they returned to New York. "Ayond, I am feeling guilty to be here and not informing the Guardian of our arrival. I think he has the right to know, after all we are trespassing on his grounds. He does not have to come and meet us." Ashtok said with a human onus.

"Guilty conscience, I did not expect a highly intelligent android to have that attribute. Okay, contact him but discourage him from coming over, we don't want to distract him from his responsibilities." Ayond suggested politely.

The Guardian was surprised to have Ashtok visit at a time when the New World Order was to convene for the year's closing session with all the member countries attending.

"Just tell me where you are, I will join you soon and don't you worry about my work, all in good hands, I have an excellent secretariat to look after it." The Guardian said.

"I told you so, it is perhaps too late to dissuade him."

"Ayond, he knows what he is doing, otherwise he would not waste his time."

Some hours later the Guardian arrived. Ashtok and Ayond went out to greet him.

"You have taken a great risk in landing here, sooner or later someone is going to crash onto the ship and have the whole community in an enigma frenzy," The Guardian warned.

"I have put a force shield around the ship that would repel unwanted guests, harmless but will keep the nosy one at arm's length. We will be here just for few days and the chances are there will be no visitors." He looked at the truck parked behind his car, "What is that big truck doing out there?"

"That contains all the materials you asked me to collect, I thought might as well deliver them as you are here and take them back home."

"How are they packed? Must unload them first and send the truck away before someone spots it and cause unnecessary exposure."

"In cartons and labeled."

"I will send some of my crew to drive it into the ship, it easier to unload in here away from peeping eyes."

While the task was being done, they conversed. "I don't know what prompted you and Ayond to visit unannounced, might as well attend the closing of the New World Order's annual closing session starting day after tomorrow, members will be happy to meet you,

"My visit is a private one, not to be announced to anyone. I am on a sightseeing tour with my dear companion Ayond. To enjoy the earthly festivities of Christmas and New Year celebrations. Also to visit some of the best tea growing areas. Then we are gone," Ashtok said.

"What is so important to visit the tea growing areas? There are better sights to see," The Guardian said in a confused tone.

"I am going to have a tea garden of my own on Urna, our earth friends and some others would relish this extraordinary plant. As far as meeting the members, it has to be some other time, an official visit with an official agenda. Meanwhile, stay here, leave early the day after and update us with the current affairs."

"Nothing pleasant, after we corrected the situation on the renegade Middle Eastern nation code name TB68, some countries have shown resentment and tried to defy our authority. Corrective action was implemented, some have complied, while some have shown rebellious threats. Even those who have complied are doing so out of fear not for the love of coexistence. I don't foresee a bright future for what we are trying to achieve"

Ashtok's response was philosophical, "For many years I lived on this world as a stationary entity and was addressed as the Supreme High, did all your thinking but never had a chance to see the outside, it was you who made me an entity capable of mobility, superior to any living being, not influenced by emotions or empathy but perform justly. I want to enjoy being alive. At the same time try to understand the human mind better, despite our assurances to create harmony to live in peace and progress technologically to fight disease, poverty and bring about amity to all mankind, yet they prefer to spend trillion of their money on warfare machinery which can subsequently wipe them from the face of this beautiful planet. This world is loaded with nuclear arsenal, if they are leashed, who will survive to be a winner?"

Ayond promptly answered, "None, but if there are any, they will fight again, at that time with bows and arrows."

The conversation lasted for hours when Ayond got up and excused herself, "I have to get some sleep not like you two who don't know what is like to be tired and exhausted."

The day came when the Guardian had to return to conduct the New World Order's annual closing session. Ashtok and Ayond accompanied him for the ride, they arrived minutes late.

"I am late, they must have started without me, thanks for accompanying me, the driver will take you back, will see you the day after, then we go hunting for tea gardens," The Guardian said with a thump of his hand on the back of the car. The car drove off and the Guardian began to walk towards the building when suddenly there was a loud explosion followed by another. The Guardian ran as fast as he could towards the car which had just dropped him. The driver seeing the commotion reversed fast and opened the door for him to get in and raced away. All sat stunned and in silence. The car stopped a little distant away.

"Had I arrived minutes earlier I would have been a pile of twisted metal," The Guardian said in a calm voice.

"And had I accompanied you, we both would have been pieces of junk," Ashtok added calmly.

"Driver, please take us back to the ship," Ayond said then added, "Who could be behind this, the loss of life of world leaders and all in that building. Must find out who is responsible for this horrendous act, definitely to disrupt what we are trying to achieve.

Back at the Avenger's clandestine headquarters, the Master and his seven accomplices toasted with champagne their successful destruction of the New World Order headquarters with everyone in it, including its head, the Guardian or at least they thought so. "Good riddance to bad rubbish. I have decided not to activate those bombs in other capitals. What the world had seen is sufficient, just a warning would suffice to remind them of the consequences." The Master said, lit a cigar, dragged a few puffed and let out a cloud of smoke. He continued, "None of our partners and friends heads of states were present because we warned them not to attend and were represented by their ambassadors, poor souls. Sacrificed for a good cause. The rest of the world will know who is boss now, not that piece of metal that called himself the Guardian," The Master said and added proudly, "We the seven partners will divide the world and rule it, with me as the head. You all come from different parts of the globe, each will be accredited to a specific zone, South America, Africa, Europe, and so on. Unfortunately we have none for North America, but as our headquarters will be in New York we may not need one." He concluded with a cheerful applause.

The television news showed the remains of the New World Order building, a pile of rubble, and confirmed the death of all inside it.

"This will surely bring back the aliens from Urna to investigate and perhaps bring in more aliens to rule our planet," The broadcast added.

The Master scoffed at the news broadcast and defiantly retorted, "They would not dare, because we will turn the western world into a rubble."

While television was showing the graphic scenes of the incident, it suddenly went blank, moments later a closed fist sign appeared followed by an announcement, "We are sorry to interrupt this programme, we have just received instructions from an organization calling itself the Avenger, whose logo is on display on the screen claiming responsibility for the attack and soon to dictate its term to replace the New World Order to govern the world." A face appeared, it began, "On behalf of the Avenger I will read out its message which is being broadcast live worldwide, 'Obey our terms or your country and its people will be annihilated like the scene some of you may have witnessed. Those who will join us will prosper, no more alien denomination. Any super power which tries to interfere with us, will not escape our wrath. We planted miniature deadly explosive devises in all strategic locations and government buildings. Do not try to find them because the moment we are aware of your prodding we will detonate them. Obey and prosper with us. Continue to function within your borders as you please, but do not make us angry because it will give us a chance to brighten your day by our fireworks. There will be further update in due course."

Ashtok, the Guardian and Ayond sitting in the spaceship heard the broadcast. They decided to leave for Urna, leaving the Guardian behind to live solitary in one of Ashtok's smaller ships, in its invisible form, giving the Avenger the pleasure in believing his demise. He was instructed to stay until such time a plan is worked out for their next move.

Before leaving they toured the best tea growing areas, Sri Lanka, India, Taiwan and China. Ayond negotiated and purchased shoots and took notes on growing and preparations.

CHAPTER 12

Back on Urna, Ashtok thought of the atrocity committed at the New World Order building with the loss of many lives. He had to make a final decision, a solution to eradicate hostilities and bring the human race to live as a family without their old habits of bickering; either by peaceful means or force or leave them alone to face their own destiny. Twice they were saved from major threats in recent years, from an asteroid that would have caused the extinction of all life and an unfriendly alien reptilian race who had taken control of the planet by hypnotic spell. (xi) A new treat had risen, the Avenger, an autocratic power had enslaved the globe. "I love that world for its beauty and cannot let it go to waste." His thoughts were interrupted by a call from Ayond. "Your annual address to the people of Urna is about in an hour. Meet you at the Administrative Council Building."

He began with brief history of their world's lucky survival when it was jettisoned from its binary system thousands of years before, "Your ancestors experienced the worst, a lesson was learnt and made those who survived understand the value to be alive, put away whatever differences they had and concentrated in building this home we call Urna after our miraculous entry into this solar system. After our ordeal in space, the planet was in a depleted condition, people lived in underground shelters for a long time and laboured hard to make it what it is today. The satellites reflect and enhance the sun light giving us the comforts of a tropical paradise. I am reminded of the people who made me, they too concentrated their efforts on improving the environment, the results were astronomical and they reached the zenith. You are no less. Your ancestors lived with me and the few while we were on Earth happily settled there, but had to leave due to social unrest which could have been corrected by force, many innocent people would have suffered, we decided against it and left." Ashtok paused, then continued. "We are happily settled here but do have a responsibility to look after our former home, Earth.

"I will put it bluntly. The humans have not learnt to live in harmony, they suffer from what you may call a kind of racialism, not of the colour of the skin or features, but due to inherited cultural upbringing which is linked to many factors. In brief, they prefer to go back to the tribal system. Large established nations break up into ethnic entities. It is very infectious. All want to possess weapons that can destroy millions and some have embarked bravely on space travel. There is a kind of a virus in some of them which has to be treated or eradicated. I am saying this because we live in the same solar system and we don't like noisy neighbours. Events taking place right now are alarming. Will do our best to bring sanity by peaceful means, failing which I will act." He concluded.

Ayond sitting with her earth team heard him with dismay. "Can't question him, perhaps the recent events in New York triggered his thinking." She said to them. As they were leaving, perhaps Ashtok had felt their uneasy thoughts about what he had said in the meeting. He walked up to them and suggested to meet at his residence the next day.

The following day, they all gathered as requested, Ashtok began immediately coming to the point. "Yesterday I may have sounded harsh and unforgiving, the atrocious act against the New World Order Building and the loss of life have propelled me to a decision fit to put things in order. I am only referring to those who are responsible to derail our efforts in creating a harmonious coexistence. Talk to them in their modus operandi language, violence with violence. Then embark to set fresh rules for humans to behave. If that fails we shall resort to harsher treatment. I will consult with the king of the Jinn, after all they too share that world being the first inhabitants of the planet. That would be my final act on Earth, but before that I must complete waking Mars.

"I had asked the Guardian to collect items of human contribution in various fields from the dawn of history to present day which he has very meticulously performed, that would take years to sort out and enrich our libraries and museums. I have chosen David to head that department assisted by Jim and Saeed the Egyptian. They had worked in museums back home and are professional in that field." He looked at David and Jim, "What says you?"

"Ashtok, we are happy with the assignment, on one condition, don't miss us out if you have an interesting sojourns in space. That would be an added knowledge to our profession."

"Agreed."

"As for Daniel, you are well connected with our wise elders bringing a better understanding to the meaning of life, and what they have achieved to enkindle the spark in living bodies to breakaway and wonder into domains not yet understood fully. Perhaps paving a way for the emergence of a new form of life. Daniel, you were a priest back home, doing the routine accepted theatrical acts to tell people what is good and bad, which actually meant nothing. Anyone could have told them so, forgive me, I am not being rude, but the people you addressed were mentally ignorant, listening to legendary tales. You believed in what you said. Here on Urna people have passed that stage thousands of years ago, they are wiser and understand the truth. Your accomplishments here are beyond belief and I commend you. Your wife Fiona would be attached to your field of work in the research. Ashtok said.

"Sam and his wife, Aishtra the Jinn will always be on my side with Ayond. I can't forget her loving care for me when I was a metal cube, though my position was the Supreme High the de facto ruler of our world, Ayond's treatment was as if I was a living being. Thanks to the Guardian who reshaped me to be a living entity. Ayond and her team started it all, with their wisdom and loyalty we have covered new grounds. For that reason I shall always treat them as an integral part of all we do, shall make or break any disorderly state of affairs within this solar system which is our home. We will be the master of all we survey, justly and wisely. We will feel like Gods, but it will not be so; that concept is earthly. In two months' time we will visit Mars again and show you what we have achieved in its acclimatization. After that, those assigned to the duties I have delegated shall proceed as directed.

"Now go and enjoy the coming festivities which we call 'Argoshtak' (xii) starting next week. On second thought, why not meet at Ayond's beautiful terrace under her grand tree and spend a few hours watching the start of the event. I will arrive just before dawn to watch the beginning of the change of colours that will surround our world for three days. It is a phenomena that happens once in three years, where it comes from and where it goes is still an enigma, our scientists have not yet been able to explain."

Ayond took up the challenge to host the occasion. Prepared her open terrace with exquisite breakfast arrangements with a display of her Victorian style china, cups, saucers and tea pots. Close to the trunk of the tree which had spread it branches like tentacles, a chair and a coffee table was set for the chief guest, the Supreme High. On the other side of the terrace, tables and chairs for the other guests.

Ayond's earth colleagues arrived early and were seated comfortably. Ashtok arrived with three attendants carrying bouquets of the most colourful flowers. They gave one to Ayond, and the other two to Aishtra and Fiona.

Ayond exclaimed, "Where are these from? Haven't seen such lovely colours and variety on Urna."

"Do you think you are the only one who can boast of having a garden? Wait a few months when I will also expand it further to include the ambrosia you call *tea*."

They were interrupted by the entrance of a line of four attendants carrying steaming kettles and plates and headed to Ashtok's table. One placed a large empty bowl usually used for serving soup. Another placed two empty oval shaped plates, the third poured into the bowl hot steaming water and the fourth threw in a dash of tea leaves and mint into it and placed shoots of tea and fresh leaves in the empty plates.

On the other side attendants dropped tea leaves into the decorative ceramic pots and poured in steaming water, while some placed other paraphernalia, milk, sugar and breakfast nibbles. When done the attendants left.

"Ayond this whole show is like a page from a nineteenth century novel. How invigorating," David remarked. The rest just stared blankly at Ashtok to begin the festivity.

"Thank you all for coming and making this occasion special." Ayond said and turned to Ashtok, "The steam from that bowl has all the flavours to inhale, the shoots and leaves in the plate are to taste. That's the best I can offer a machine, forgive the pun." She said with a bit of humour.

While enjoying the calm atmosphere and early morning breeze, only the sound of empty cups or spoons being placed on the saucers filled the stillness.

Argoshtak began to announce its presence, mist began to form, gradually thickening to envelope the entire planet. Streaks of parallel lines with the colours of the rainbow began to form. Just then the pale rising sun peeked over the horizon, it rose wielding its luminosity but dimmed by the mist and colourful lines that encased Urna. They all walked away from under the tree to an open area to witness the transformation. Moments later, the tint of the miasma changed to light grey and the steaks of parallel multi-coloured lines became more prominent. They began to drift westward. In its middle a large oval shaped like a buckle in a belt started to take shape, inside it, purple cumulous formation churned with defused lighting strikes. They waited until it settled down after completing a circle of the globe. Minutes later it started to move again to repeat its revolution.

After several hours Ashtok excused himself, "I must leave you now, wish you all the joy and happiness. May the coming years bring prosperity to our world as always." With those words he left.

Shortly after the rest also left leaving Ayond fully stretched under the canopy of her tree.

On the third day, hours before the culmination of the enigmatic performance of colours, David and his colleagues arrived at Ayond's home.

"There are already some good signs of flowers budding and fresh leaves all around," David remarked as they assembled watching the gradual fading of Argoshtak.

"I can't understand it, in so many years experiencing this miracle, no one has been able to decipher its origin or purpose, not even Ashtok the super ultimate computer," Jim said almost talking to himself.

Daniel heard him, "In this vast universe there are perhaps more such miracles which we humans or even non humans like Ashtok, the ultimate computer cannot figure out. There must be a higher power that understands and gives…." Fiona made a sign not to indulge into matters that may not be acceptable to others.

Aishtra looked at Fiona, "Let him continue, it is refreshing to hear what some think. May not necessarily acceptable, let his mind speak loud to relieve his inner thoughts."

"Thank you Aishtra, we humans are always afraid of what we think or say that others may find offensive. It is because of ignorance…" Daniel stopped seeing Fiona's disapproved expression on her face. He decided to leave. She ran after him, "Sorry Daniel, none of that from me in future, I promise." She said apologetically.

CHAPTER 13

David, Jim and Saeed busied themselves with the unpacking of cartons containing books, scientific research documents, films and documentaries of scenic landscapes, photographs and works of art and the list goes on as Ashtok had requested the Guardian to collect.

"A fortune must have been spent to acquire these, I wonder why this sudden interest in transferring these to Urna, they are better off on Earth, why deprive it from its heritage," Jim questioned.

"No one question the Supreme High Ashtok, only he knows the answer." David said thoughtfully.

Saeed murmured something to himself, "What was that you said?" Jim asked.

"Perhaps he foresees a catastrophe where these would be lost," Saeed said.

"What catastrophe can happen and wipe out all the museums and libraries." Jim paused and added, "Unless he foresees a world war that will reduce humanity to the Stone Age."

"I was thinking of that, but is it possible for a war to do so much harm?" Saeed asked.

"Of course, with the thousands of nuclear bombs the super powers and others possess, both side can have a wonderful display of their muscles forgetting that in the process they will outdo each other and pave the way to extinction, and if any are left, they would ponder, 'what have we done?' Their answer would lay in the smouldering ashes which would tell the story of once a thriving humanity flourished and now buried in it."

"You have a sadistic view Jim, this cannot happen, God would protect the good." Saeed said.

"By whose definition you consider who is good or bad. God may have a different weighing scale, something in the line of your Book of the Dead. What you may consider good may be different from God's point of view. You and many live in a dream world. For thousands of years your people believed in a doctrine of after life and even in the twenty first century still continue to do so, though some have changed their views. All said and done face the truth, politics and religions, if they continue as practiced would perhaps be the main cause for the ultimate disaster. You are backing the wrong horse, wake up," Was Jim's casual comments to a lost in thought Saeed.

"It is getting too complicated to think anymore, let us leave it at that." Saeed said shaking his head.

Meanwhile Ashtok busied himself to fulfil his commitment to Europa's aquatic inhabitants. He sent a team of marine biologists to study the plant-life in its vast under the ice ocean. There were plants like algae, lettuce ulva and kelp, similar to those found on Earth with the exception of one which grows like a creeper spreading along the sea floor and has instinct to prey on other plants and marine life.

They also confirmed Ashtok's assumption about bacterial species that don't rely on sunlight, live by using chemical energy derived from minerals and chemical compounds from vents to convert carbon dioxide into sugar.

"The similarity in marine plants is a close cousin to the ones found in the Martian sea, the creatures would relish Europa's harvest which is more nutritious. But the living plant/animal creepers would pose a problem." Ayond pointed out.

"On the contrary," Ashtok said, "I think it to be a blessing in disguise, it will keep them on the alert at all times and reduce the element of aggression on the docile kangaroo like beings, if threatened they have the advantage to lash out their strong sonar ripple waves and their high frequency clicks the Martian creature cannot stand. With such a weapon the Martian guests would realise their host's uncanny ability and in due course the two species will hit it well. As far as the hostile living plants, it will keep them distracted."

Work began with the planting of more herbals and the introduction of lower form of marine life. The Kangaroos 'watched' or better still felt happy with what was being done. Months later the harvest was inspected and the results were commendable.

It was time for the Martian marine creature to be transported. Ashtok accompanied by Ayond, her colleagues and a squad of marine experts arrived on Mars. They sat at one end surrounded by dozens watching as the divers entered the waters with sting guns and brought in immobilized sea creatures, placed five in a large transparent container. It was arduous but meticulously handled, loaded on to vehicles and transported to the ship. There were three hundred and seventy two creatures including infants. Among the spectators who joined in much later when the operation was near completion, were the Elders, the teachers, Akak and Joshua. Before he could ask what was going on, Akak just said, "I will explain to you later."

The Elders thanked Ashtok for getting rid of their predators. They were assured all have been removed and will be comfortably housed in their new home and were promised that the squad of mariners will return to double check if there were any left behind. Other underground lakes will be checked for the presence such creatures.

The Gentle Stream parted with its load of marine creatures to Europa. The submarine *Fiona* had a limited hold capacity, several trips had to be made from the main ship to the ocean below near about the area where the Kangaroo like inhabitants lived. It was a long and tedious ordeal. Ashtok and his companions watched on the screen the marine squad removing the new residents out of the water bags and woking them up. In a daze they floated sluggishly, swam aimlessly. The mariners had stun guns just in case of an aggressive encounter. The creatures were in a stupor not knowing where to go, the drug effect was wearing off gradually. Realising the change of location and the taste of water, they let out high frequency calls and gathered. Instinctively, perhaps a sign of uncertainty they began to disturb the grit on which they stood with their tentacles turning the water murky.

In that commotion, plant/animal creepers stealthily began to wrap themselves on to some of the Martian creatures, instantly they were ripped, torn to shreds and swallowed. The tumult attracted the Kangaroo creatures, they began to gather at a distance. One approached the Martian creatures and sat on its tail. The water in front of it began to vibrate sending long spread waves. There was no response from the other end. The waves changed to ripples, moving faster with a slight whine. Still no response. The ripples became more successive with stronger whine, and the Kangaroo companions joined in. The water around them vibrated and the whining bellowed. The Martian creatures began to droop into a state of hopelessness by dropping their appendages and moving side to side with moans.

The Kangaroo creatures may have understood their moan-call of surrender and stopped their whine. One of them moved forward, and began to sprinkle the sand. Not understanding its purpose there was no reciprocal response from the newly arrived guests. Instead they moaned unanimously and began to blow water bubbles with a low pitch murmur. A signal of stress understood by their hosts who reciprocated with a similar hum. One of the Martian creatures sluggishly sauntered forward muttering. The Kangaroo moved towards it and were almost face to face, the host bent over and scoped some grit, threw it randomly, a sign of welcome. That action was repeated several times. The message it conveyed was finally understood by the new arrival, in turn reciprocated the same way. Then, almost simultaneously both uttered a loud whine, repeated instantaneously by all the assembled creatures. That may have been a signal of mutual trust, both creatures mingled uttering soft whines and parted.

Inside the *Fiona*, Ashtok commented, "All parties involved are happily settled, a job well achieved. I leave you to ponder on how those two creatures or beings who are so different from each other came to a peaceful settlement to live together. It shall always remain a mystery as to how they communicated and understood each other, what did they say by those clicks, murmurs, hums, water ripples and bubbles. It must be a form of sounds or vibrations only water species understand. Perhaps our fish and whales have that vocabulary. "Why don't humans take a lesson from them?" Ashtok wondered.

"Perhaps the marine lifeforms don't have a large jargon to jabber, come straight to the point." Sam put in sardonically.

"The recording is an educational piece, must be preserved for our museum collection," David suggested.

With joy and satisfaction *Fiona* surfaced and flew back to orbiting *The Gentle Stream.*

Back on Urna, a message was delivered to Ashtok. He read it and said, "We have just solved one problem and another has risen, some of our Oxygenators are over heating due to deficiency in our power source and had to shut down. This will cause delay in the environmental enhancement of the Martian atmosphere. A cooling system has to be made which will take about a year. In addition to cooling, their exhausts were contributing an added function to enhance the greenhouse effect. Because of this, our plans to start construction of the first domed city would also be delayed. But the work on pipes from the underground water supply and the filtration equipment will continue as scheduled."

"Ashtok, with your guidance and wisdom we will have them running, a little delay would not make much difference, we have been working these machines for years and many times in the past they were problems which were solved it." Ayond complimented.

"Thank you, Ayond what I like about you is your optimistic approach and by the way, I have decided to name the first domed city after you, and shall be the capital of that world. You will christen it, other cities would bear names from our world and Earth."

Ayond was left emotionally dumb struck. With tears in her eyes, she looked up at Ashtok, "I don't deserve it, when I die just a tomb stone with my name would suffice."

"I have decided, your contribution on Earth, Urna and Mars is unequalled in our history and I can't think of anyone would qualify better to have that honour. Subject is closed." Ashtok said using a finger gently wiped off the tears off her eyes.

Days later on Urna, Ashtok asked Ayond to accompany him to visit the library and museum on an inspection tour to see how David, Jim and Saeed are managing with the countless materials collected by the Guardian. "It will takes us months if not years to catalogue and label these, but when done, the people on Urna will spend a life time reading them. We are leaving some empty shelves for any future additions," David said very proudly and continued to work.

Ashtok in his mind wondered if there would be any more worthwhile additions forthcoming, "Perhaps half a shelf would suffice," he said in low voice pessimistically.

"We may have a problem in the future with the recorded discs, it would be advisable to convert them to play on your machines as the earth ones may not last very long." David pointed out.

"Once your job is done, I will arrange for it." Ashtok said.

After they left, David felt odd about a remark Ashtok had made. He drew Jim aside, "What do you think about what he said, 'leaving half a shelf would suffice'? The way he said it, I felt that he was not too enthusiastic, he just shook his head and murmured in a negative manner. Either he is no more interested in adding to the library or perhaps he is not expecting any worthwhile contributions forthcoming."

"David, he is all knowing, he must have a reason to act that way, unless he feels he has had enough of that world …." Jim was interrupted by David.

"Or there will be no one to contribute as the humans may have done it." David said calmly.

"Done what?" Jim exploded.

"Blow themselves, trigger a nuclear war that would end it all." David replied in a pathetic tone.

"It is possible, we have had two world wars in the twentieth century and a kind of proxy world war which is still happening in twenty first century. On two occasions it could have triggered a nuclear confrontation, but sanity prevailed. We are now in the middle of the century and tempers continue to get out of hand despite the guidance and control of the New World Order. Who knows, we humans love to play with fire, that trait would never go out of our system." Jim said coolly.

"From the age of ignorance to the present day we humans always found an excuse to fight whether in the name of God or religion, territorial gains, economic or just an excuse when you don't like the face of someone. In a nutshell a kind of a sport, to conquer and rule. It is no more when armies stood face to face in an open field but now it is nations and even continents can be blown to smithereens. Neither the Guardian nor Ashtok with all their powers can stop it from happening. In the past, the gods people worshiped must have shown their anger and punished the wrong doers, those were localised events, but now the story is different, it is no more regional but global. If they are watching, as Ashtok is, perhaps one of them will strike the final blow" David said.

Jim just shook his head.

CHAPTER 14

Space programmes on Earth were limited to the moon, Venus and Mercury, fearing a reprisal should they go the other way towards Mars or the Jovian planets. The report by the astronauts of Mars-3 mission was kept away from the public. Mars was out of bound as far as they were concerned.

The authorities suspected the aliens were responsible for the booting out the astronauts and could do nothing about it. The Guardian who was living in seclusion in an invisible spaceship somewhere on an isolated hill top was kept informed by news broadcasts.

Ashtok addressed the Administrative Council on Urna, headed by Ayond. The earth team attended as observers. "The defective Oxygenators were replaced and the rejuvenation process on Mars is progressing satisfactorily. The time had come to start the work on building the first domed city, which will be called 'Ayond, the capital city of planet Mars. Other cities will have names of people who had and are contributing to the progress of our world."

"Excuse me Ashtok," David raised his hand. "What about a name or two from Earth?"

"David, I have not finished. I have about fifty names, will select some of them, my even select from you people. There will be many domed cities.

"As I was saying," He continued, "In a few hundred years or so the planet will be flourishing, I want to make a 'Utopia' of it. Earth would have been an ideal place, but not meant to be. A paradise lost with all its natural splendour, beauty and gifts of all kinds of life, sadly its residents don't see it that way and perhaps will bring it to an untimely demise.

"Just to satisfy your curiosity David, some of the names I have chosen include great men and women, like Abraham Lincoln, Plato, Galileo, Nightingale, Curie, Beethoven and many more. So be rest assured your former home will be represented adequately. In the foreseeable future Mars would be a flourishing planet, with multi-specie occupants living side by side outside the domes.

David stood up and humbly said with a bow, "Ashtok our Supreme High, I and my colleagues are so thrilled to hear it from you."

"Thank you all, before we finish, I would like you all from now on to address the Martian Ants as Marants, a name coined by Ayond, the head of this council.

"So be it." Ayond endorsed happily.

That evening the team assembled at Sam's residence for Fiona's birthday celebration. Music and refreshments took charge of the occasion.

"It is like back home, does not matter where we are, as long as we are happy, *that is life*." David said and raised his glass. They all followed and tunefully Sam said with a loud voice drowning the music, "Happy Birthday Fiona, may you live forever in this beautiful land. Cheers!"

Fiona modestly responded, "Thank you all, and especially to my husband Daniel without him I would not be here."

Sam burst again, "And a big cheer to Daniel, bottoms up everyone."

The rest of the evening they talked about the council meeting earlier in the day, "I wish I could live that long to see Mars' transformation, at least for now I will have a chance to live in the first domed city, though I prefer Urna." Jim said mildly.

"None of us will live on Mars, it will be just visits to assist the new comers to adjust. Our home will always be Urna." David put in.

They were interrupted by a call from Ayond, "I am coming over to wish Fiona."

On her arrival more refreshments flowed, at one point she requested David to play Mendelssohn's violin concerto. "That piece always inspires me to speak my mind. With you people I found solace of a different kind, with my people it is different. I can't explain why. You are more vibrant, you know how to enjoy life when you want to."

"Why Mendelssohn so special," Jim asked.

"That is a long story, when he was a child his family were not in a comfortable state and it happened we were in the area and felt sorry for them. We extended help and without their knowing gifted their son with tuning his mind with the knowledge of music. You all know what I mean."

"You mean infused music in his head?" Jim asked.

"Yes, you may put it that way, we have done it several times on others, not only music but other faculties like the sciences, engineering, architecture, arts and many others. That's how you got some of the brilliant minds."

They partied the whole night.

Meanwhile, Ashtok sat alone at his home watching old silent movie and comedies of the early twentieth century. He was deeply engrossed when suddenly another screen came to life and the Guardian's face appeared.

"I hope you have something pleasant to tell me, you have interrupted my concentration." Ashtok disliked to be interrupted while watching his favourite shows.

"You couldn't be concentrating more than I being in isolation for over a year now, though inactive, have my ears open to any broadcasts that may interest us. The Space Agency has just announced that a mysterious object has been sighted many billion miles away and it is heading towards our solar system. They said it is globular in shape, could be a large asteroid or a planetoid, its shape is a bit unusual. You can check it out at your end. I will keep you informed of further development. Before you go, how long am I going to stay in seclusion, how about my returning to Urna?"

"Stay where you are, it is important we have a presence there."

Ashtok called Urna's main observatory to check on the approaching object. Hours later, confirmed a large cylindrical body travelling with an enormous speed. Not an asteroid but a spaceship of some sort. He instructed them to watch its progress and to keep him posted. About a month later, he was informed the ship had begun to decelerate.

An emergency meeting was held with Urna's Administrative Council. "We have been watching its progress, it has decelerated which confirms its intentions to come to this solar system. Whoever is in there perhaps knows about Earth being habitable, Urna will not show as it is always covered by Jupiter. They could be hostile, it is imperative for us to intervene and check them out. The ship is very large and it is not an ordinary one, from its size and shape it must be carrying a lot of cargo, perhaps an army and a lot of weapons, if so that is serious. On the other hand, if friendly we will spread the red carpet, using earth's terminology. Here on Urna, our defences are adequate to repel any aggressor, but I fear for the people of Earth, they will not stand a chance, their weaponry is good for regional bullying and defences, not for an invasion from space. From its trajectory there is only one possibility, coming from the binary system of Alpha Centauri, which is 4.37 light years away from our sun. We never found any possible life on any of its planets, unless…" he paused for a minute, "Unless there is a planet hidden away by one of its suns in conjunction or opposition.

"Heading for our solar system only means that they have made a study of its planet, found life and perhaps occupy other planets or moons depending on the biological structure they are made of. We had the bad guys, the Xanthumians a reptilian specie (xiii) who lived on Jupiter's moon, Io and frequently visited Earth when they got a chance. Now we have another enigma, what kind of planet would suite them, they have a variety to select from."

"Their ship may not necessarily be carrying an invasion force, could be just innocent civilians wanting a new home." David reasoned.

"That is also a strong possibility. In any case we have to be vigilant, my ship has all the amenities to handle the situation and we have sufficient time for our rendezvous with those visitors and for the safety of the solar system." Ashtok said.

CHAPTER 15

The observatory on Urna advised on the decelerating speed of the mysterious space object. Ashtok sat with Ayond and her team. "It is clear that it is a spaceship and calculating from its position and speed it is heading for our solar system and the estimated time of arrival is about two months." Ashtok explained and added, "We are going to meet whoever they are. Prepare yourselves for another long ride."

Weeks later, they boarded *The Gentle Stream*, Ashtok addressed his passengers, "Our visitors are close enough and it will take us ten Earth days to intercept.

On board you have the luxurious accommodation and entertainment facilities to spend your time. Only during the start and prior to our approach to meet with them you have to be confined to your seats just for a few hours during acceleration and deceleration time. During that time, look out and see how the stars flash past you as we go and come to a standstill when we stop. That should keep you occupied during those durations. Any questions?"

"Any idea how to communicate with the visitors?" Sam asked.

"I have no idea at the moment." Ashtok said.

"How about a drawing of a hand shake." Fiona suggested.

"Suppose they don't have hands and misunderstand the message, on their world it may mean something different, perhaps something obscene." Jim interjected.

"Why are we speculating, let us first reach and the situation at that time will dictate what is to be done." David advised.

On the eighth day of their journey, deceleration sequences of *The Gentle Stream* began and came to a halt miles from the approaching visitors. Reciprocally, the visitor's spaceship, slowed and came along side, its shape was unusual, three long and wide cylindrical structures joined and tapered to a point, dwarfed *The Gentle Stream*.

"That is the oddest looking ship I have seen. Let us hope its occupants have a more pleasant feature." Sam commented.

Fiona meanwhile had prepared a sketch of two hand shaking with an interrogation mark and passed it to Ashtok. Obligingly he took it and transmitted it.

They waited for several minutes for a response.

"I hope they can understand it," Fiona said softly.

"They are probably taking their time to figure it out." Sam put in.

"It is so simple, a child can understand it." Daniel said.

"They are not children from Earth or Urna, What if it *is* an offensive gesture in their lingo and don't respond?" David asked.

"That is their bad luck, we will send another one to show a sketch of their ship taking an about turn." Ashtok said.

While they were debating what action to take, a message flashed on the screen.

A caricature of a smiling face with the words in English, '*You must be joking*'.

Stunned by the message, Ayond promptly typed a reply, "You mean to say that you can communicate in English, who are you and where have you come from?"

In an instant a voice replied, 'Is that the way to treat people who want to get back home?"

"What do you mean by back home? Which home? Ayond asked

"Why of course, Earth."

"How is Earth your home, and you are coming from the opposite direction?"

"No point in scribbling and talking on the screen, it is a waste of time, come over to our ship and will explain all you want to know. Bring you ship alongside the area highlighted by blinking lights in the shape of a door. A bridge will be extended."

"Pleasure to come aboard, but first show us what you look like." Ayond asked politely.

"I said to you that we are returning back home, we must be human."

On the screen a human face appeared.

"How do we know that is not a photograph or an image? Show your entire form and some hand movements."

A handsome man of about forty came to view, he waved a hand in greetings and said, "How do I look, good enough for you?"

They were stunned to see a handsome male figure. "A good looker." Ayond commented.

The Gentle Stream maneuvered and came along side. A bridge connected the two. Ashtok and Ayond were the first to walk across and enter, on the other end the man who appeared on the screen extended his hand and shook theirs. He introduced himself as the captain of the ship and gave his name as Zathenfur.

Ashtok greeted him, "I am Ashtok the captain of my ship, very happy to be on board your ship captain Za- ta-fur."

"It is difficult to pronounce my name, it sound like this, Zetafur, the letters h and n are difficult to pronounce if you don't speak our dialect, consider them as silent." He looked at Ayond, "I presume this is your wife?"

"No, not my wife, this is Ayond my deputy."

"Please bring in the rest of your family."

They all walked in and each shook hands. When shaking hands with Fiona, he held her hands a little longer staring at her face.

"These ladies and gentlemen are work colleagues not my family." Ashtok explained.

"Before we sit, let me take you on a tour of our ship.

"How many people do you have on board?"

"Six hundred and thirty seven including the one just born minutes ago." Zathenfur replied and added, "Where we are standing is the bottom level where we have smaller crafts and workshops."

They moved up from deck to deck until the fifth level. All occupied by people, milling around and a school with children. They entered a large room with infants, each on a bed encased in a see through material with a monitor above each showing the face, name, date of birth, weight and a number. "They will stay here until they reach the age of two years by your calendar, then released to their parents. During this period the child is visited regularly by the parents."

"Very impressive, it is like a city, looks like you have well planned your exodus wherever you came from and must have been travelling for a long time. You have catered for all the amenities so as not to feel you are in space. I have also noticed that all your signs are in English." Ayond pointed out.

"When I tell you our story, it is unbelievable how our race had survived jumping from one world to another. One more item I want to show you before we settle down. They got into an elevator. "We are now going up to the top level."

On stepping out Sam exclaimed, "Can't believe what I am seeing, this place is like a large garden and the roof top is high up, transparent and globular, it is just unbelievable."

Zathenfur led them to different patches of vegetables and fruits. "There are only two persons attend to the garden. The watering system, temperature control and the occasional spray of nourishing chemicals are all automatic, there is one person to supervise their functions. Now I take you to my favourite spot." At the far end, plants with multi-coloured flowers of different shades exhibited their allure. "Without this we would lose our sense of beauty."

They went back to the elevator and got off into a corridor and entered a room fully furnished, lined up with glass cupboard stacked with books. Artifacts of different sizes and shapes displayed elegantly.

"I cannot imagine we are in a spaceship, like being on solid ground," David remarked.

Please be seated ladies and gentlemen," Zathenfur politely pointed to the chairs.

"Before we start, let us have some refreshments, you must be tired, unfortunately we don't have your beverage of alcoholic drinks, but have a simple one, we relish it and keep us reinvigorated, we call it *tshee,* may be difficult for you to pronounce it, just consider the 't' is silent. From where you come it is called tea."

The word *tea* hit an electronic nerve within Ashtok. Ayond and the rest couldn't believe what they heard.

"Did you say tea?" Ashtok asked.

"You have tea on this ship?" Ayond asked.

Zathenfur was unsure of their reaction, perhaps it meant something offensive. His response was mild and explanatory. "Yes, don't have anything else, it is a drink made from a plant, sorry to disappoint you."

"On the contrary, we love tea." Ashtok replied.

"It was the only beverage my ancestors brought from earth and has thrived throughout the ages. There are five varieties, each taken at different times and moods."

Just then an attendants entered with a large trolley, lined up with cups and a tea pots followed by another with a host of snacks. They served each person on a small table besides them.

"These are all vegetarian, so help yourselves," Zathenfur pointed at the dishes.

When the attendant was about to serve Ashtok, Ayond interrupted, "Excuse me Mr. Zathenfur, our captain prefers to enjoy his tea in a different way, on a plate a few stems of tea shoots and tea leaves would do. I will explain when your attendants leave."

Zathenfur slightly confused, "I see, your captain is a fussy one, wants to sample it before indulging, an expert tea drinker." He instructed the attendant to comply.

"In a way yes, but also incapable to take it as we do, his metabolism is different." She explained Ashtok's physical form and ended by saying, "He is not human."

Their host more confused and before he could speak the attendant returned with a plate stacked with what was ordered.

"Let us enjoy the tea then we can talk." Zathenfur politely invited. He watched discretely without focussing on Ashtok going through his ritual of relishing the shoots and leaves.

Ayond added, "Besides being our captain, he is the highest authority in our world."

"You mean on Earth?"

"Not Earth, but our planet Urna."

"Never heard of it, where is it, I was under the impression that you came from Earth."

"As you claim to be from that world, must be familiar with the solar system and the planets in it."

"I am familiar with all the planets, perhaps you mean Mars and have a different name for it."

"Not Mars, but close to it, sandwiched between Jupiter and Saturn and we are also associated with earth.

"Forgive my ignorance," Zathenfur said politely, "We, nor our ancestors ever heard or seen such a planet. It does not appear in our records."

"Well let me tell you how we came to be in this solar system." Ayond began, "It is a long story, in brief, our planet once was part of a family in a binary system, due to an anomaly between the two suns we were hurled out and drifted in space for a long period of time, until by chance entered this solar system and were added to its family. That was about fifteen thousand years ago. Some of us lived on Earth and made it our home. How can you be from there, we would have known about you and would have seen it develop technologically but no traces of such activity. Kindly explain, the only way I can look at it is that you are aliens from some part of this galaxy and may have visited it, but that too does not make sense because we would have known of your presence, unless such a visit was made before our time." Ayond concluded.

Zathenfur listened attentively and said, "Strange you mentioned that Ashtok is not human. I am reminded about reading of an incident much before my time, well recorded in our archives, someone like your captain slightly different in colour but close in resemblance visited us, spent some time with our scientists, told them he had nothing more to offer and left never to be seen again. It became a legendary tale, some speculated that it was a supernatural omen to check on our achievements, being satisfied he left. We have a recording, will show it to you if you wish."

Ashtok guessed who that visitor was. "That person was perhaps made by me from the world I originally came from." He narrated how the people who made him resorted to use robots and artificial intelligent androids to run factories and the affairs of the community to make up the dwindling population due to sterility. When all living beings died out, there was no use for the androids to stay, and were sent out to find new homes where they can be useful. "One of them must have visited you, realised your technological abilities and no practical purpose for it to stay. However, to cut the story short, as Ayond has explained we lived on Earth for a long time and I do remember meeting some highly advanced beings very different from the local population. They claimed to be living there much before we had arrived. (xiv). So it must have been your ancestors.

Ayond was beginning to get the thread of events. "How about telling us your story Zathenfur."

He began, "How strangely this jigsaw puzzle is unfolding. Some twenty thousand years ago when humans or better still Homo sapiens were getting a foothold and traversing across continents, our forefathers came to a world from a star in the Orion Constellation. Our sun was perhaps the closest to yours and had three planets, two gas giants and our planet.

"Our world is much older than the Earth, thrived with life with highly advanced technologically. An irreversible climatic change occurred, unbearable to sustain, eventually all life and plants began to die with no hope of survival. Our ancestors filled as many ships as possible and left. From the records Earth and an uninhabited planet in the Alpha Centauri binary system were their two choices, preferred the former, embarked on a journey of about twenty six light years by your time scale. They had the technology to travel at enormous speed which builds up gradually so as not to feel the effect, in about a year or so reaches the maximum velocity, millions of miles per hour. The journey took generations, but they made it.

On arrival they had no concept of living on land as the only world they knew was the spaceship. Spent months on the ship orbiting, surveying the landmasses, humans were crisscrossing all over and chose an uninhabited area. It stretched from Central America eastward, short of the West African coast, the sea in between was infested with sharks of many varieties, some were deadly giant creatures. That was a barrier that discouraged the crossing over to colonise the land, an ideal place to settle down away from any interaction with the locals."

"You have such vivid recollections of your history," Ayond commented.

"It is all recorded, thousands of years of documented history. As I was saying, that virgin continent was what you may call a paradise. Evergreen, cascading streams, lakes, a variety of herbivores animals and birds of different colours and shapes. The diversity of fruit unimaginable, sweet as honey and very nourishing. A mountain range ran in the middle. Homes were built, land were cultivated. A central power station ran our factories and provided domestic lighting, a complex power source not yet understood by your scientists, only referred to it in theory. You may have an inkling, but not know what it is, it took us many years to harness it.

"Their new home was as good as could be, at the same time the spaceships were regularly maintained, ready for any eventuality. Kept a vigilant eye on the human activity mainly on the land east of them. We did not bother them nor did they bother us. Several thousand years past without an incident, but then minor quakes began to be felt throughout the entire continent. The seismologists kept a watchful eye. A major quake shook the entire landmass but there was no serious damage."

Ayond interrupted, "I can guess what had happened."

"Please let me finish, I am going to tell you, or better still show you something that may interest you." Zathenfur said and got up, went to a cupboard, spent minutes searching. "Got it." He said and walked back to his chair. Between his thumb and index finger he displayed a small spherical marble and inserted it into a niche in his arm rest.

"Ladies and Gentlemen, let me surprise you," he paused and looked at Ashtok with a smile, "We had met before, correction, not me but my ancestors long time ago."

Ashtok was listening attentively, he had made a guess.

On the screen spaceships landing on a green fertile land close to a river, an aerial view displayed the confluence of five rivers." That is where your people landed Ashtok, in the land what is today Pakistan." Zathenfur said coolly and paused the image.

"No, it can't be. Do you really mean that they saw them land?" Ayond said excitedly.

"Watch a little more." The screen became alive. Scenes of preparation of make shift habitats surrounded by locals who watched in awe at the heavenly visitors from the sky. Some approached with wooden trays stacked with variety of food, bowed and exited humbly. "They surely must have thought you all are some kind of heavenly beings, which was the reason for their generous gestures." Zathenfur commented humorously.

No reaction from Ashtok as he remembered those times, though he was then a cube form, a machine moved around by the Guardian.

Zathenfur continued, "Sometime later, for some reason unknown to us you packed up and moved a few miles south in a less fertile plains close to the river. There you built homes with water and drainage systems. You were happy, but why did you leave the granary of the north?"

Ashtok remembered it all. "There the hospitality of the locals was getting out of control. Every now and then, offering of trays of food and buckets of milk were brought, we tried to explain that such a diet does not agree with us, but it went on deaf ears. We had surveyed the area and chose to settle in a place no one wanted to go to, a barren desert, which we made livable."

Zathenfur continued, "Your move made them suspicious, unsure of your intentions and decided to make contact. Our seniors were met by an android, similar in resemblance to you Ashtok, he took them to a talking machine. At first it thought they were like the locals and feared their intrusion, but then they explained their story and made a request that they should not be contacted and be left alone. The machine said to them, "You are guests of this world as we are, live your lives without any interference from us and likewise do not interfere with ours." He looked at Ashtok, "Does all this rings a bell?"

Ashtok calmly said, "I do remember it well as if it was yesterday. Your ancestors were more advanced than most in the Milky Way Galaxy and had chosen well to come here. The land your ancestors lived on was one of the best from all aspects, but unfortunately the entire land mass was unstable. Plus the influence of the miles deep accumulation of ice on the neighbouring continent was affecting the weather. We wanted to caution them but had stuck to our agreement as they had explicitly dictated not to be contacted. Had they asked for our help when the catastrophe struck we would have given it and would have found a suitable area for them to settle down. Had they stayed, together we would have shaped a world better than what it is today. That was not to be. Please continue with your narrative about the events that led them to abandon this world."

Zathenfur continued, "Quakes became more frequent, suddenly a large chunk of the western landmass connected to Central America sank below the ocean. Our scientists predicted more land would go under due to tectonic activity. Our seniors debated on asking the new comers who came from another world for their assistance. Suddenly a large volcanic eruption occurred in the north followed by a quake that shook the whole continent, it began to buckle and break. They knew the end was eminent. No time to waste, decided to leave. Their spaceships were kept ready well in advance in the event of such an eventuality, a lesson learned from their ancestors. Very few could make it, the rest were left behind to meet their fate, to be swallowed by the sea or escape by boats to the east or the west whichever was closer. Our destination was to a planet close to Proxima b in the habitable zone of its star Proxima Centauri which is about four point two light years away. That was the planet surveyed thousands of years earlier, the choice between it and the Earth. We named it Sparka."

Ashtok explained that in that binary system, only Proxima b can be seen, no other planet in the goldilocks zone.

Zathenfur pointed out, "It is in an elusive spot, cannot be seen from here, perhaps like Urna tucked away behind Jupiter, however, they lived there since. The planet had two continents, one large and the other very small, both surrounded by an ocean. More than half of the northern and southern hemispheres were ice locked. The weather was moody, seasonal hot gales melted the ice and the water level rose, almost drowning the smaller continent, on the larger one they lived further inland away from the coast lines. For thousands of years they lived comfortably. Just about a few centuries ago a change in weather which would melt the ice set an alarm. Just in case of an emergency situation, the spaceships were kept ready and waiting. But when disaster comes, it does not knocks on any door, it beaks it open then announces itself.

"My great great grandfather was a skeptic. He was the captain of one of those ships, and had always argued with the authorities to leave before it was too late. Nobody paid any attention to him. However, on his own, discretely stocked his vessel with all the needs for a very long journey. He had sounded his family members and close friends for such a situation. A year later a spell of hot scorching fast winds played havoc all over the planet, the ice began to melt, the water crossed the danger zone, he alerted the would be passengers. Without attracting any attention they walked into the vessel without any baggage, the essentials were stored beforehand. He and his crew secured the ship and took off. The authorities could do nothing to stop or communicate. They were distracted by the rising water level. By the time emergency was declared and efforts to load the ships were made, ocean waves surged and lashed mercilessly drowning whatever was in its path. The ships remained embedded in a watery grave. Their broadcasts of the disaster were recorded."

"Very interesting, how accurately you have explained it as if you were there." Ayond commented.

"My great great grandfather recoded it all in the log book and had it not been for his foresight, I nor any of us here would have been alive."

"Excuse me Zat…f," David began but could not pronounce his name.

"Za – th – fur, that should be easy, what have you to say?"

147

"Nothing important, but if I may, could I have another cup of tea?"

"Gladly, we will all have another round."

After the tea was served, he continued, "I am the fifth generation captain on this vessel. My parents started me from the lowest position rising up to being a captain. About a hundred years ago we started to receive radio and television broadcasts. Through a British educational children's channel we learnt the alphabet and how to make words. We made it compulsory to converse and communicate in that language to make it easy for us to merge in our new home. The signals took years to reach us, but kept us informed and we knew what was going on. Humans have reached an age of enlightenment, we are certain to receive a grand welcome, especially when they get to know that we were there before. That is our story in brief."

Ashtok thought for a while before commenting on what they believed their welcome would be like. "True, Earth was your ancestral home once long ago and have the right to return to it, but things have changed, not too sure how welcomed you will be. For a short time your people will be all over television channels and perhaps will provide you a living space, but in the long run your people will feel the claustrophobic environment, not in the sense of space but in attitudes. The human race is unpredictable in many ways. Sorry to say, in some ways it is not as enlightened as you think. You can go and try your luck but the chances are you might have to leave and start another search for a new home."

"I cannot understand what you are trying to tell me, a discouraging attitude, worst come to worst find us an island in the Pacific, we have to settle down after such a journey." Zathenfur said sadly.

"The people in general are good, but there exists under current motives which diversify and lead to chaotic behavior. Humans in many ways cannot tolerate each other and resolve their disputes by the use of force, surely you would not like to be caught in those squabbles. The absence of respect for human life is the order of the day. To bring sanity we embarked on setting up a governing order whereby all could live in peace and harmony, but it does not seem to work. I have a suggestion, for the time being avoid landing there, be our guests on our planet Urna. I am sure your people need to rest after so many years in space. It is not as big and beautiful as the Earth but we will make your stay as congenial and comfortable as can be. We are developing Mars to be habitable, you would then have three choices, stay on Urna, leave for Earth or share our endeavour on Mars." Ashtok offered.

Zathenfur thought for a moment, "You are not making it easy for me to decide, an offer of three worlds to live on. From your words I sense a genuine gesture of care and goodwill, I chose to be on Urna, but have to consult with my people."

"I have a question for you Za- th- fur? You mentioned your people learnt the English language through television broadcasts, that is incredible, but the familiarity with expressions and habits goes beyond me?" David asked.

"Very simple, once we learnt the language we tuned in to many other broadcasts, news, serious and comedy shows, we watched as part of our education rather than for entertainment. It was compulsory. From childhood we grew in that environment, we became part of that culture so to speak, to merge comfortably."

"A very creditable foresight by your forefathers." David acknowledged appreciably.

149

Shortly after Ashtok and the rest left and waited for Zathenfur decision.

It was not a long wait, Zathenfur came on the screen, "Captain Ashtok, I have discussed the matter with my people and they have unanimously accept your kind hospitality on Urna."

"We are pleased with your decision, I will come over with some of my crew and discuss the flight plan." Shortly after they met and planned the speed and trajectory, straight towards Jupiter.

On *The Gentle Stream* on an occasion while Ashtok was strolling along the upper deck found Daniel pinned to a window admiring the countless little dots of light that streaked by, forming the embroidered tapestry of the void. His thoughts were running wild, on seeing Ashtok he murmured loud enough for his approaching companion to hear, "What *heavenly being* has created all this."

Ashtok simply said, "I had been told another version of this by the people who made me back in my original home planet. They said something quite different from what you are thinking, whether theological or scientific.

"It was simply explained, the universe was vacuous for billions or trillions of years or perhaps for an indefinite period of time. During that long period, particles of some kind began to form very much like an aqueous material floating undisturbed in one direction with a positive charge and from the opposite side a similar substance with a negative charge, separated by the vastness of empty space. How those particles materialised they did not know but theorised the possibility of two collapsed universes. However, the two substances approached each other as if attracting one another, until they collided. In less than a fraction of a second the two charges permeated causing a capillary action right across the vastness of the universe tearing the substances into countless shreds and fragments that created the infinite state of what we have today, the cosmos."

"But who created those two substances and if they were part of a collapsed universes, how they came to be and who or what created them?" Daniel asked.

"Daniel, you have scored, I have no answer. Can go on for ever guessing who or what created the original source that started it. But one thing for sure, as a result of the positive and negative charges we have the male and the female in every application of life. Of course these are just hypotheses, one day we will have more enlightenments, and that day may be after eons when beings will be gifted with the ultimate knowledge contained in the universe."

Daniel was about to say something when Ashtok said, "I know what you are about to ask, shall we leave it for some other time."

A crew member came up to Ashtok. "Excuse me captain, you are wanted on the bridge."

"Daniel, I have to go," he said and left.

At the flight cabin Ashtok was told they were approaching Jupiter and decelerating. Instruction were given to Zathenfur to do the same. In a matter of hours both vessels were orbiting Urna.

Ashtok advised Zathenfur, "Your vessel is too large to land, a special site will be arranged, we will ferry your people by our shuttles."

CHAPTER 16

Months passed, Zathenfur and his people were settled comfortably. Ayond along with her team and many from Urna routinely met and familiarised them with local customs. In the beginning it was slow and frustrating. All their lives they had lived in a closed environment, were not used to open spaces. Fiona once commented, "Like a bird who spent its entire life in a cage and suddenly is let free. At first it would prefer to return to its cage as that was the only world it knew. With time it would learn the meaning of freedom and may never return. The same applies to these people. The element of uncertainty exist, and they move around suspiciously and unsure, though glad to see their children adapt well and are happy with their schools as compared to the ones they had on their ship."

"Give the elders some more time, they too will adjust well." David said.

Zathenfur and some his colleagues became attached to Ayond and her team.

Ashtok busied himself with the Martian project.

While on a visit to the museum where David was in charge, Ashtok and Zathenfur came unannounced. David welcomed them but excused himself, "Forgive me I cannot join you as I have an important matter to attend to. Feel free to peruse around."

While walking around Ashtok put a question to Zathenfur, "You never once mentioned the name of the land your people lived on for so long on Earth, was it not called Atlantis?"

"We did not have a name as we did not need one. From earth broadcasts we heard of that name for the first time and I am sure none who escaped to North Africa and Central America ever mentioned a name. It must have been created by those who listened to their stories and referred to them as the people who came from that ocean. The Greeks perhaps coined that word," Zathenfur explained.

"Very possible, what about any documents the survivors may have carried with them?"

"That is possible, some of our architects, scientists and map makers must have saved whatever they could carry."

"All must had been lost or laying on a shelf with someone who does not understand its significance."

The two moved on from one section to another stopping occasionally at artifacts examining them. Just before completing their tour Zathenfur's eye caught a glimpse of something that looked familiar to him. He darted to it while Ashtok stood and waited. He waved his hand without turning around. Ashtok joined him and stared at a simple looking figurine of a female which was purchased by Ayond many years ago from an antique shop in Egypt. An odd looking design of a female with raised hands and both feet joined at the ankles.

"You seem to like it. What attracted Ayond to purchase it was the facial expression. The red fiery eyes and the way her hair is flying in all directions as if facing a storm."

"Quite so, it is not her looks, it is what it can do, it is very special. What if I told you, this figurine is a special key to unlock the most powerful energy source you can imagine? We have used it on applications where power was needed, even in Atlantis. Strange to find it here. This one must have found its way to Africa by someone special who was entrusted with it. Normally with an individual in the hierarchy to activate a mechanism. He must have been one of those who managed to reach Egypt."

"What mechanism are you talking about?" Ashtok asked.

"Can't explain right now, but if you would be kind enough to bring it to my home, I will show you what it does," Zathenfur requested.

The next day, Ashtok and Ayond were at his home.

Zathenfur led them to a room. From a vault he carefully picked a metal box and placed it gently on a table. On the side of the box facing them was a panel with some unknown letterings. He touched a few and waited. The panel lit and the letterings changed. Again he touched them. Waited a few moments and there was a click, the lid gently rose opened. With both hands he removed what looked like a ball with a stalk connecting it to a circular base.

Zathenfur requested Ashtok to insert the figurine into the vertical cavity niche in the stalk. He did. On top of the ball a square shaped blueish light materialized. Seconds later around its centre a belt of orange light began to blink and the ball started to rotate.

"What is it," Ayond was baffled.

"An enigmatic power source. Not mysterious to us anymore since we discovered the source of it, a power so great that exists freely throughout the universe. It took our scientists many years to harness it. Can be applied to wherever and on whatever function where power is needed. Used commonly in our homes and factories, even running our ships. Do you know what it is?"

"No." Ayond said.

"It is freely available throughout the Universe, you refer to it as dark energy and we call it *neumarak,* in our language means 'life giver'. We had a problem in storing it, took our scientists many years and many lives were lost but finally succeeded. This ball has enough energy to light a city. No wires are needed to transmit, it is in the air like the radio or television signals. Just put up your bulbs or any equipment and they will work, of course with a simple receiving mechanism." Zathenfur explained then added, "Unfortunately some such balls must have sunk with the land mass you call Atlantis and an active one which was powering our facilities must be still functioning and emitting signals randomly as the key or the figurine like this one is still inserted. Any electronic devises in the vicinity like ships and aircrafts would disorient their functions and bring disaster. A bad situation, but hopefully it has not done any harm. Those without the figurines are harmless."

Ayond thought of the mysterious happening in the so called Bermuda Triangle. She could not resist saying, "So you the people of Atlantis, are the cause for the infamous happenings out there in the Atlantic Ocean. Though not your fault, can it be stopped from emitting those signals?"

"That energy never dies, it keeps replenishing itself. Some day when we visit Earth, I have a device to locate it and remove the key." Zathenfur said.

"With all that knowledge, had your people stayed there instead of leaving after Atlantis sank, their contribution to the development of the human race may have been different."

"Agreed, had my ancestors moved to some remote island instead of roaming in space like gypsies it would have been a better decision. Well, what was done cannot be undone. Let us look ahead and see how we benefit mankind by it. With the guidance of Ashtok we can apply it more usefully."

"Zathenfur, I would not think about mankind right now, there are many problems there and we are trying to sort them out. But it can be useful to something more important. We may need more than one of these."

"We have some and can produce more, we have the technology. Each has an indefinite life, keep on regenerating automatically. An example of that is the one at the bottom of the Atlantic Ocean."

"Zathenfur, you and that device you call *neumarak* are truly life givers. We will sit again and explain to you where I would like to use it."

Not long after they met and Ashtok explained the Martian project. Zathenfur was thrilled and requested to visit the planet.

Soon Ashtok and Zathenfur accompanied by some of their technicians left for Mars and toured the underground factories producing oxygen, other gases and enhancing the greenhouse effect to stabilise the climatic change. Finally they visited the site of the first domed city. "You may select any location for your people, we will build it and name it whatever you like."

"Very generous of you, my people would come for short visits to enjoy a change of scenery but I am sure they would prefer living on Urna."

On their way back to Urna, Zathenfur advised, "It would not take long before the entire planet is energised, your machines would work more efficiently, more than many folds of what they are now. Also will benefit the entire planet where ever electricity is needed, including the domed cities. We will also install some on Urna."

"I can foresee a great future for your people and ours. Your contribution will go down in our history books, and you can name your city *Atlantis* if you prefer. We will have cities named after some good people and places from Earth."

"You and your friends must accompany us at the time of installing this miracle power." Zathenfur suggested.

CHAPTER 17

The Guardian had miraculously escaped being minutes late in entering the New World Order Headquarter building when two bombs shattered it killing all who were inside. To give an impression to those responsible that he was among the dead, continued to live in seclusion in one of Ashtok's small invisible crafts somewhere on a hill top. More than a year passed, he kept vigilant on the brutal administration of the Avenger and his accomplices. Extortion, bribery and unjust imprisonments had put the entire world on the edge of collapse.

The Guardian made a call to Ashtok. "The Avenger rules with an iron hand. He applies what most humans understand perfectly well, deal force with force, perhaps he will do a better job than us. The Avenger and the whole world are under the impression of my demise. Unless you have a plan to get rid of these bullies, there is no use for me to stay here, I wish to return and help on the Martian project."

Ashtok thought for a while, "A sad situation, we cannot surrender the people to the mercy of a psychopath dictator. Give me some time and I will contact you shortly. I may have some plans to entertain the so called Avenger." Worried he called Ayond.

"We cannot do anything as long as those bombs are planted in strategic locations. We would be risking many lives. How about asking Zathenfur if he has any suggestions." She advised

Zathenfur proposed to neutralise the bombs, "You mentioned that in his broadcasts the Avenger threatened to detonate the devices if someone tried to fiddle with them, it only means and I presume they are triggered electronically by the press of a button, perhaps from a central command location, connected with a close circuit television to monitor them. If so, I can deactivate the connections by sending negative sound waves that would cause the circuits to dysfunction. But has its drawbacks, in the process all electronic devices all over the beamed area will also be non-functional, including communication systems, aircrafts, ships and trains. You have to discretely warn the airlines, ships and trains would just stop in their tracks. All will come to a standstill so long as the negative waves are switched on and after achieving our goal, will be switched off and life will return to normal."

"Sounds good, but what if it does not work or conversely turns the world topsy-turvy not knowing what caused it. The Avenger will surely suspect sabotage being cooked up and in vengeance will set off a number of explosions causing unnecessary loss of life." Ayond observed.

"That is a risk we have to take. The explosive devices must be small to fit in unsuspecting places and the frequency by which they are activated is as simple as sending a sending a telephonic message. I am sure of our success." Zathenfur assured.

Ashtok listened to their conversation attentively and gave his approval. "I suggest for the start, since the threatened places are mainly in Europe and North America, let us first concentrate on those area."

"Good idea, we will use two crafts, one for Europe to beam down the negative waves and the other for North America." Zathenfur suggested.

Accompanied by Zathenfur and Ayond they arrived on Earth in their invisible spaceship, stayed a hundred miles above New York. Ashtok asked the Guardian to fly out and meet them. They sat and discussed the plans. The Guardian was given the task to contact his undercover security men in various capitals to go and stay at a safe distance from some strategic location. They were relieved to hear from him, and got to work right away. Within hours they reported back, all was set. One of them found the location of the Avenger's headquarters and the names and the addresses of the accomplices. Ashtok was more than pleased. "Now I can kill two bad birds with one stone." He told Ayond.

The Guardian contacted his men to inform major airlines and the air forces in Europe and North America to suspend all flights effective from six hundred hours the following morning until further notice. The authorities on their own discretely advised private flying clubs and sensitive government agencies.

From several hundred miles above the Earth two spaceships were in position, Ashtok's with Zathenfur above Europe and the Guardian in his smaller craft above the North American continent. Both to beam down the negative sound waves simultaneously.

"I just hope there are no bombs planted in other locations outside these two continents for the Avenger to take revenge." Ayond pointed out.

"The Avenger's broadcasts only referred to the capitals of the western world. That is a chance we have to take." Ashtok said.

Zathenfur contacted the Guardian, "Sixty seconds count down for you to activate the beam. Keep it on until you hear from me."

People on the two continents were at a loss to find their cell phones giving a weird sound when switched on, television screens displayed murky hazy lines, ships and trains electronic equipment became non-functional, and electric connections were disrupted. Life had come to a standstill. The public were alarmed and in a number of cities and towns church bells rang and many awestricken men and women flocked and headed to the ecclesiastical venues.

Some hours later, Zathenfur requested the Guardian to ask some of his security men to check on strategic locations where bombs were planted which they had earlier discretely located. They were asked to retrieve them. Suspenseful minutes passed. All reported back the successful removal without any mishap.

The Guardian informed Zathenfur who exclaimed, "Great, we have done it!"

Satisfied with their achievement Ashtok said, "Now for the final act, to wipeout the Avenger and his companions once and for all."

Meanwhile, at the headquarters of the Avenger a report came in about the grounding of the airlines and non-function of electronic equipment. The Master became suspicious and as a show of power decided to activate a few devices randomly in some capitals. He asked his accomplices who were in his chamber to watch the screen for some firework display. "I don't like it, someone is responsible for this disruption, I will show them, it does not pay to play the fool with me." He went to his desk, switched on the monitor screen, it displayed fuzzy jumbled lines. He instantly exploded with curses and furiously uttered, "I will show them what I can do meddling with me." The Master hotly looked down at his keyboard, randomly punched the keys. The screen remained unchanged, continued to display the same fuzzy images. He was unsure if any detonation had occurred. Still in a fit of rage, using both hands, thumped on the keyboard, muttered vulgar swears and declared looking at his accomplices, "I will blow all their cities and turn them to rubble."

"Master, how do we know if the bombs were detonated? The screen is dead, can you ask someone to go and check." One of partners said.

"I will do better than that, call the airport and ask one of my pilots to fly and bomb some cities randomly, only then those responsible for sabotaging my television system will bear the consequences and understand the extent of my anger." He picked his cell phone and punched the numbers. A strange hissing sound buzzed in his ears. He was mad and angry, again using filthy abuses and curses, flung the cell phone across the room and shouted for security.

Meanwhile, Ashtok's invisible vessel had descended to fifty feet above the Avenger's headquarters. Through a loudspeaker a voice called, "You, the Avenger come out and meet your nemesis. Show your strength to me if you can" It kept repeating and the voice was getting louder and louder. The security staff were baffled, could not see the source of the voice which was coming from above. They hurriedly reported to the Master, who along with his collaborators came out. The loud ear shattering calls continued. The Master looked up towards the direction from where the voice was emitting. Not seeing any visible source, yelled with fury and threatening hand gestures. "Where are you, why don't you show yourself, you coward and who the hell are you?"

The voice from above came back, "As I said, I am your nemesis, have come to send you to hell along with your supporters." The vessel materialised in full view and began to ascend gently. The shocked onlookers below began to scatter and run in all directions. From above a lethal thin beam of light scanned the complex and its surrounding area melting it down to a mushy pile along with all its occupants.

The negative sound waves were switched off and life turned to normal. Newspapers and television broadcasts blamed the strange anomaly to the electronic devices and bizarre electric glitches on unprecedented sunspot flares. The Guardian flew back and parked his tiny vessel in the hold of *The Gentle Stream*. He then contacted his security men on the ground, informed them of the Avenger's eradication and to contact television stations to receive a broadcast to be relayed through satellites in two hours' time for a special transmission to the world. To their relief, they complied promptly.

The Gentle Stream in its invisible form flew and remained stationary some hundreds of feet above the middle of the Sahara desert where for miles all around there were only sand dunes of different shapes and sizes. Television screens across the world were switched on, they were told of the elimination of the Avenger by the New World Order and shortly a special broadcast was to follow. The suspenseful world audience waited.

Ashtok's face appeared, a new face to them, "My name does not matter, an entity who has wisdom and compassion, the Guardian whom you know and is the head of the New World Order represents me, he has requested me to address you. I am not a politician nor a deity, but someone who wants you to live in a happy and comfortable world. To achieve that we have set rules to monitor its application impartially and justly. Those who disrupt its functions will face my anger and to demonstrate what it would looks like, I have chosen this barren portion of the Sahara desert where no one can be hurt. Only a fraction of this display eradicated those monsters who called themselves the Avenger."

Television screens displayed the vast emptiness of a desert landscape, serene and lifeless, with the wind caressing the sand dunes sifting gently its upper layers. The afternoon sun looked down exhibiting its might. Suddenly as if a door opened from hell sending flaming tongues down that snaked above the sandy landscape, bellowing on contact and bursting upward with a blaze reaching high up and swaying like fiery pillars in a macabre dance, accompanied by loud crackling rumbles. The cauldron of hell fire display sent shudders to the viewers. It lasted for several minutes to allow the effect to sink in. A powerful chemical spray instantly extinguished the inferno.

Ashtok came back on to the screen. "That is just a small sample of what I can do. You must have liked that act of violence as it is in your nature to relish scenes of horror and pain in films and stories, as long as you are seated comfortably in your homes or theaters. Unless there are scenes of violence, you do not enjoy them. Think for a moment, imagine such an event is actually happening to you, would you like it? Give it a serious thought.

"Let me tell you, the Guardian who is in-charge of maintaining law and order also possesses such powers, do not make him use them. Soon he will be addressing you. I will be keeping my eyes on you from somewhere up there. Your leaders know that we once lived and shared this wonderful world for fifteen thousand years, but decided to leave when you resorted to live in a chaotic state. We only returned after saving you from an asteroid that would have turned the entire planet similar to the demonstration you have just witnessed. Having done the good deed, we rightfully inherited the custodianship of this world. (xv)

"Let me take this opportunity to give a brief background of what we have tried to achieve when we lived here. Initiated means to bring harmony and peaceful coexistence for all, to dissuade the imposition of bigoted ideas that brought about miseries and prejudices to millions of your fellow beings. Continue to believe in them if you wish, but in a personal capacity, do not force them down the throat of others. That I will not tolerate.

"Some may remember, over two decades ago the insults my representative received at the United Nations which resulted in our leaving you alone to deal with the chaotic state you were in. Despite what had happened, ten years later we destroyed an asteroid heading your way which would have extinguished all life. We returned to tell you that we gave you a new lease on life and found an old alien reptilian adversary robbing your gold and had put a hypnotic spell to control you. We got rid of them. Today we eliminated the autocratic Avenger, rescued you from yet another catastrophe. Three times we showed our genuine intentions to help you. Had we had no love and affection for the human race and your world, we would not have bothered. So please adhere to the New World Order, in the long run you will realise its benefits and prosper.

"A word of caution to some, and they know to whom I am referring, not to indulge in economic gains or political supremacy using your muscles or faiths as means to an end. Those are old tricks, during the past thousand years lands were conquered, millions slaughtered, properties confiscated, women and children were taken as slaves, all in the name of God and country. Don't get me wrong, I have nothing against your faiths, do as you please, but do not forcefully subject to submission others who are different from you. Remember, I am watching every move you make.

"When we lived on this world we did not interfere with what went on, good or bad. Only a few knew of our existence here. Now the story is different, we are your custodians, have inherited the guardianship of this world by virtue of saving it from total disasters, not once but three times in a very short time. This planet has become our responsibility to keep it safe and alive. I will give you one more advice, may have referred to it earlier. Use your good faith as it dictates to be better citizens. Don't bother if other are different, each individual is responsible for his or her salvation, you will not be there to defend or accuse on judgement day, so why bother. Don't get me wrong, I am not referring to one or two faiths but to all. Perhaps a wise leader will emerge from an area more complex in these conditions, to bring change for the better and spend generously paving an exemplary way to govern. That would perhaps be a lesson to others.

"I have taken this opportunity to address you all personally to establish a pledge, just follow the governance of the New World Order and you will be happier than ever before. Those who break the rules will pay heavily. I may address the world body with all the heads of nations and reaffirm what I am saying. If you are still wondering about my name, I am the Supreme High as I am called in other worlds. Now I take my leave and wish you a pleasant future."

Ashtok's face faded and normal broadcasts resumed.

The world was stunned and wondered who that person was. They were familiar with the Guardian, but he was different. Some welcomed him as the messiah who will ultimately bring sanity to the world after the treacherous behaviour of the Avenger. Some called him god in disguise who will bring prosperity and justice to their lands.

Ashtok, Zathenfur and Ayond returned to Urna, the Guardian was asked to stay behind until further orders. On the way home, Ayond put a straight forward assumption, "I wonder how some may have felt what you philosophised about their faiths."

"My dear Ayond, my most trusted friend, remember I am not made of flesh and blood, I am a machine with artificial intelligence, have no compassion for what humans or other forms of life think of someone hidden away in the universe who made them and in return worship Him, and for their good behavior will give them eternal life in a place they call paradise. I believe in cause and effect. And, come to think of it, I am helping them to be good and ease their path to that paradise, don't you think so."

"Well, if you say so, but…" He interrupted her.

"No buts," He looked at Zathenfur "What have you to say, I want to hear your views on the subject?"

Zathenfur thought for a moment, "I am not a machine but flesh and blood, another form of life, I come from billions of miles from your world, once very long ago we believed in a supernatural deity, a belief developed out of fear not love. In due course with better understanding of the mysteries of existence and higher scientific knowledge and understanding we gave up such myths and legends. In brief, I believe in what you are trying to achieve."

Ayond did not look very pleased, just said quietly almost to herself, "So be it."

Somewhere in Eastern Europe a man calling himself *The Interpreter* walked the streets claiming that he guessed who that person was who called himself the Supreme High. "He appeared out of nowhere and what he demonstrated in an instant, with the snap of his fingers made the desert turn into a flaming hell, perhaps a view of it. I strongly believe that voice was of god, not appearing in a form and distract the people to spend unnecessary prostrations and the theatrics of worship. Fellow citizens of the world, hear me well, obey his representative who calls himself the Guardian, perhaps he is an angel in disguise."

He kept repeating his message over and over again. At some point he was pelted with tomatoes and eggs, but that did not deter him. His words reached far and wide. Newspapers just called him a lunatic old man. He became the topic of conversation among all walks of life.

The Guardian fearing for the old man's life from fundamentalists and religious fanatics, sent an emissary and discretely explained to him. "The Supreme High and the Guardian are not supernatural, just people like you, more or less, you are talking like a person from the past ages of ignorance. You must stop your antiquated blabbering. You mean well but take our advice, stay indoors for a month or two and people will forget you. This is an order from the Guardian.

CHAPTER 18

Ashtok and Ayond decided to introduce Zathenfur to the Martian Ant inhabitants or the Marants as it was agreed to call them. They were greeted with their form of courtesies and were given a tour of their habitat. Before they left Zathenfur requested to be photographed with them.

On their way back to Urna, they conversed. "I am fascinated by the way they live and understand all what that goes around them." Zathenfur said.

"Ashtok began to explain, "Many thousands of years ago when we first became part of this solar system we began exploring the planets and the moons around us. It was during those expeditions the Guardian along with some surveyors spotted something odd on the surface of Mars. A lifeform was mending what looked like a hole on a mount. They looked like a species unknown to us, more like enlarged insects, with unbelievable dexterity.

"When they eventually met them, they were cautious and suspicious but when we offered to help develop their living quarters and provide them with some of our teachers to educate them in all fields, they willing accepted. It took many years to reach what you saw today. According to them, this planet was lush green and supported many forms of life. An unprecedented shower of meteorites and fiery electric charges were the causes for turning the planet into a barren waste. Their habitat were mostly underground where water was plentiful. On the outside, conditions were intolerable, perhaps similar to that experienced on Earth when an asteroid slammed on to it sixty five million years ago nearly causing the extinction of life, only insects and lower species managed to survive. The Marants are dexterous, perhaps some elements in their biological make up that made them endure hardships and adjust to environmental changes. They will be an asset to the development of Mars and will share some of the domed cities."

"An enthralling story, by the way how is the progress with your Oxygenators, are they achieving better results?"

"That dark energy or *neumarak* as you call it, has done miracles. Reports I am getting are very encouraging. It shan't be long before the first signs of weather modification should appear. Once that is achieved, we can begin the habitation of the planet. While we are here, let us visit one of the workshops and inspect it to give you an up to date picture of its progress.

Zathenfur was most pleased with his visit, "I have seen it all, what you people have done and are doing is more than commendable, we are lucky to be associated with you."

Back on Urna, happy with the achievements, Ashtok asked Ayond to host a dinner for Zathenfur, some of his colleagues and her own team.

They all gathered and the party was in full swing. They danced, exchanged jokes and some sat in groups talking.

Zathenfur saw Fiona in the distance and darted towards her. Staring at her from head to toe, he said in a calm polite way, "Seeing you the first time when you visited us on our spaceship, I wanted to ask a personal question, but that would have been impolite. But now as we have become a family, may I say what I wanted ask?"

"Of course Zathenfur, feel free."

"To be honest you reminded me of a person I knew some time ago. She was the keeper of all our confidential documents, my right hand in running the social affairs on the ship when I was second in command."

Fiona was dumbfounded and did not know how to reply him, but just said, "I may be the re-incarnation of that person. Tell me something more about her."

"Let me recollect the last moments we parted company, yes it was when there was an electrical glitch in one of the living quarters, while repairing it she got electrocuted and died instantly. She should have called one of the electricians, but being an enthusiast she took an unnecessary risk." After a brief pause with an unhappy face looked at Fiona and said apologetically, "I am sorry, please forgive me."

Fiona felt like he was apologising to the person of his past, and did not know how to respond, but involuntarily she replied, "If you think me to be that person, I do sincerely forgive you."

"Thank you," Zathenfur said and moved away feeling relieved.

David had his back towards them and heard the conversation, he turned around and walked up to Fiona, "I overheard your conversation with Zathenfur, he really thinks you are an incarnate of someone he worked with, I don't believe in reincarnation but it is possible for two or three unconnected people to look alike, besides, that must have been several hundred years ago, how old is he now?"

"May be he is reincarnated repeatedly." Fiona added with a mischievous smile.

"It is not a laughing matter Fiona, Zathenfur is not the type to telltales, there must be some explanation to him being alive and kicking like a person between forty and fifty. I have to find out, perhaps someday when he and I are in a friendly and informal discussion."

The party went on for many hours, they merged well like old friends. Conversations were on lighter and serious subjects like archeology, space, music and the arts. Ashtok was pleased with them. He leaned towards Ayond and whispered, "They have passed my test, I am confident that these two groups will respect each other and will have no problems. I foresee their contributions would be magnanimous."

"Have you noticed that all the men and women of Atlantis look between ages of thirty and fifty? There are no old people. We live long but age begins to show on faces once we reach four hundred." Ayond made an observation.

"I have noticed that, in due course we will make a complete study of their biological mechanism."

Zathenfur, David and Sam walked up to Ashtok.

"We have come to ask you, what initiated you to experiment on a dead planet to bring it to life." Zathenfur asked.

"Correction, not a dead planet. Like a plant when it loses its leaves, given the right conditions it bloom again." He continued to explain how the Guardian found the Marants which encouraged him to look into reviving the planet to be liveable. It needed a jump start and I took that challenge. In the long run, it would perhaps be an insurance to an alternative home just in case something happens to Urna. Planets, suns, even galaxies come and go, nothing is permanent, it is always good to plan ahead."

"You remind me of my ancestor who on Sparka, planned ahead and kept his ship ready, when danger was announced he was the first to leave with his friends and their families. That is how many years later we the descendants are still alive." Zathenfur said.

"Very courageous of your ancestor, things can happen most unexpectedly. Take the case of Urna, an anomaly between our suns kicked us out of the system and sent us sailing into the unknown; could have crashed into a planet, swallowed by a sun or continued indefinitely into space. We were lucky to cruise into this solar system and be part of it."

"I can't understand, you lived on Earth, why not on your planet?"

"When we entered the solar system and saw a thriving world, decided to get as many people as possible on our spaceships and landed there not knowing the fate of our planet Urna which was caught by the sun and placed into orbit. Many years later we found out, and when we made contact, the descendants of those who survived refused to accept us for abandoning their ancestors. We had not abandoned them, by the time we landed and unloaded everyone, the planet had moved far. However when we explained it to them they agreed to allow us to return any time we wished. While we lived on Earth we sent our technicians to assist in rebuilding Urna."

"You preferred to stay rather than go back and live with your own people. Why was that?" Zathenfur was curious.

"It was not for me to decide, though I was their Supreme High, a stationary cube at that time, who only did the thinking, it was up to the generations who were born there, they were more oriented to earthly condition than Urna and they preferred to stay."

Ayond interjected, "I could visualise their situation at that time, I was born there too. However it was a wise decision to stay at that time."

"Yes Ayond, you were born there, you do understand what I mean." Ashtok said.

Zathenfur thoughtfully put in, "Unforeseen predicaments led peoples from different corners of the Milky way to meet on a spot in the boon-docks of the galaxy. I am sure it is an omen for better thing to come."

"Zathenfur I do not believe in omens, but for certain, we are heading for better things to come."

"Can't dispute that, our Supreme High surely knows best, for he is the master of Urna, Earth and the life giver to Mars." Ayond added. After a pause she said in a low tone as if talking to herself,

"I wonder what will be the reaction on Earth when they find out about Mars's new look, they would certainly begin a race to plant their flags."

Ashtok promptly replied, "Not if I can help it, any attempts to land would be turned back before they would set their feet on its soil. Only we will chose who would fit to be a Martian."

The get-together went on to the early hours. The next day was a weekend.

The next day Ashtok contacted the Guardian, "From your reports all is working satisfactorily, as best as can be. Your intelligence department should now concentrate on selecting one or two young families with two children, preferably a boy and a girl from different parts of the world who would be willing to immigrate to Mars. The choice is yours, but they must not talk to friend or families of their intentions. Good men and women, and when I say *good*, I mean good, you understand what I am trying to say.

"It is time for you to announce to the world that The New World Order is in full control. Start with a smile, just joking, I know of our physical incapability, you can wave a hand or improvise any action to put the viewers at ease and at the same time stress on maintaining the peace, I shall be watching." Ashtok concluded.

A day was announced for the broadcast. For that period all offices were to stop functioning and television sets were switch on. It was a working day. The moment arrived and all were glued to their sets worldwide. The Guardian's image appeared. He gently waved a hand with words of greeting. He began, "Ladies and gentlemen I am the Guardian, head of the New World Order and the official representative of the Supreme High. Fellow friends, by the authority invested in me, I have bad and good news. Our governance is functioning as well as expected, but there are some defaulters. They will be dealt with appropriately. Hours ago we uncovered a plot being hatched somewhere in Asia with their operatives right here, in New York planning an attack on my headquarters. You will witness on your screens the punishment they and their accomplices will receive. Let it be a lesson to all. The good news is that twenty two nations have adhered to the rules meticulously, many restrictions would be relaxed to them.

"Now witness on your screens the punishment of those who think they are above the law. First those who are plotting to attack this building and are in this city. Our intelligence has located their abode."

A military helicopter hovered over an isolated farm house on the outskirts. On the ground someone came out and looked up, he ran back inside and came out with a rocket launcher. Took aim, before he could fire he was put down by a shower of bullets from the copter. More men came out and began to run, but they too met the same fate followed by the obliteration of their sanctuary. Next was to a city on the other side of the world. A small saucer shaped craft circled it, zapped lethal beams of light in all directions reducing every structure to rubble.

The Guardian came back on to the screen, "The bad guys had planned an attack on my building and the city was the home of the plotters who were also engaged into disturbing the peace in a neighbouring nation, many innocent lives were lost in the process but it had to be done. Let it be a lesson to all." With those words he ended.

CHAPTER 19

A week after his first broadcast, the Guardian came again on television. He ended with the same cautionary advice, and added, "I have received a report that some people are spreading rumours about our attitudes towards political, cultural and religious practices which are absolutely baseless. We have allowed you the freedom to do as you please, as long as it remains within your borders and not to use force to achieve it. Such reports breed dissention which could lead to violence. That we cannot tolerate. I am sorry to say, nations and persons involved in spreading those gossips will be reprimanded.

"With immediate effect the New World Order will take possession of all weapons of mass destruction from all the countries that possess them and secure the sites where they are located, only reasonable arms will be allowed for local policing. Any local disturbances of violent nature within any nation will be dealt with severely." The Guardian was brief.

After that announcement the scheming hordes were kept out of circulation. The apparent peaceful situation pleased Ashtok who could then concentrate more on vitalising Mars. The dark energy power source accelerated the output of the Oxygenators many folds. He embarked on constructing the first domed city on Mars. He invited Zathenfur, some of his seniors, Ayond and her earth colleagues and the Marants Elders to a ceremony of laying the foundation stone. They stood on an open ground with the layout demarcated. Close to the marked entrance to the city a white slab stood with the words engraved on it, 'Laid by the most precious hands of the persons who made this dream come true.' Below were the names of the attendees. Beside it in a small box a crystal artifact was placed and buried.

"That little box if ever opened in the future will have the record of who and when it was put, with pictures of the attendees." Ashtok said.

Sam asked, "In so many years will they have the machines to activate it?"

"It is so simple to operate it, in the future even a school boy would have the knowhow, so don't worry about that. Now if you follow me I will show you the layout of the city."

He began to explain, "Around most of the parameter of the residential complex there will be gardens, children's playground and a place where elders can sit and relax. The front portion near the main entrance to the city will be an open space. The entrance will have an airlock system, enter into a room, the main gate shuts and after acclimatising enter the city. Right here behind the gardens would be a large residential building split into two segments. In one, the interior will be designed to suit the Marants living style, and the other for my colleagues and I. Both will be separate and independent of each other. There will be a tunnel below, which will lead to a deep underground emergency habitat. Other cities will have similar or other facilities designed to suite the requirement of the occupants.

"This first city will be named *Ayond,* in honour of the person who guided our planet's destiny and for her achievements. She is here among us and on this note let's have a toast for the occasion." The ceremony ended with joyful songs and felicitations, the Marants Elders' appendages swarmed showing their commendation.

On the ship, on their return journey to Urna another celebrations ensued. Attendants popped Champagne bottles, the echoes sounded pleasant to Ashtok and he requested for the corks to be brought to him. He had to show his part in participating, picked one by one and sniffed, moving them to and fro. Expressionless, but conveyed the appreciation. He looked at an attendant and said, "There are times when I wish to be a human, but as I am not, can you please have one for me." The attendant gladly filled a glass, touched it to Ashtok's hand and took a sip.

Having achieved success on earth and the forthcoming prosperous future envisioned for Mars, Ashtok was delighted and wanted the people of Urna to participate. Ayond declared a holiday commemorating Ashtok's rebirth from a cube of artificial intelligence to a *living being,* "A kind of birthday." Ayond announced.

Invitations were issued including some senior persons from Urna. The day arrived and soon the festivity began with jubilation and fun. In a corner David, Jim, Aishtra and Fiona sat talking with Zathenfur. David politely addressed him, "Can I ask you a personal question that has kept me puzzled for a long time. How the people from Atlantis or for that matter their descendants live that long. You said to Fiona that many years ago you had a friend who looked like her on the spaceship you have been travelling for hundreds of years, which also means that you are hundreds of years old?"

"Will be happy to tell you, it is very simple. I will start with a brief background relevant to your question. I am a descendant from the people of Atlantis as you call them, then moved to Sparka, a name given by them for a planet in the Centauri Binary system. They had to leave due to the weather change, it was getting unbearably warm, fearing the melting of the polar ice would ultimately drown the landmass, decided to return to our former home, Earth. Many years later while in space we received radio and later television signals, though the transmissions took some years to reach, we were kept informed of what was happening there. We learnt from one of the documentary programmes the name Atlantis given to the continent and the people who disappeared with it. I have explained it earlier that we did not have a name, perhaps coined by learned people like the Greeks who listened to those stories from our survivors who landed in North Africa.

Anyhow, I am a descendant from a line of captains on our ship, and my age is about six hundred years by your calendar. When my father was the captain, I was second in command. I had an assistant who looked like Fiona, due to an unfortunate accident she was electrocuted, we were planning to get married. I was thirty eight and she was in her twenties, by our calendar scale."

"Very interesting, especially about your long years in space and longevity," David said.

"Let me explain to you a little bit about the world our ancestors originally came from. A binary system in the Orion Constellation, two suns orbited around a common barycenter and our planet had a unique orbit, it was locked between the gravitational pull of the two, it revolved and rotated around one and as it came in between, the attraction of the other drew it to orbit around it forming the figure of eight so to speak. Our day was long, about eighty hours of your time and our year was calculated by completing the figure of eight cycle, which took about fifteen earth years. The average life expectancy on our world is about hundred by our time scale, I am still a young man of about forty five, but by your time scale about six hundred years plus.

"Also, our biological system is different from humans. We may look like humans, which is not uncommon in this vast universe, but internally have evolved differently which perhaps aided our life expectancy, nature gave a helping hand. A unique gift of biological replacement of internal organs as we get older. For example, at a certain age when an organ begins to show lassitude automatically a replacement begins to grow. A heart, kidney or liver begins to grow and takes over their functions. The worn-out just dissolves away. The average age of our species is about fifteen hundred years by your calendar, unless we are killed in some way or by a natural catastrophe. The processes within our bodies are a natural phenomenon," Zathenfur explained.

"Amazing, you are very special people. One more question, if I may? If you can live for that long your world must have been over populated." Fiona asked.

"On the contrary, again something different from your species, our females begin to conceive only after she reaches the age over twenty five or about three hundred and fifty by yours time scale and only once in a lifetime. Produce a male or female or a third gender, unknown to you right now but perhaps in the near future you humans will have it coming."

"A third gender, what do you mean?" Fiona was confused.

"This third gender is a miracle of nature, quite unique, but easy to explain. Long long ago there were only two genders, it was not uncommon to have a child with a genital physical deformity at birth, simply to explain like what you call a eunuch in your world. Subsequently in some, not all, nature began to play a role in manipulating their internal mechanism making them hermaphrodites with the gift to conceive a child of their gender. Their off-springs are only of their own sex, so we labelled them as the third gender. They are intelligent and wise. They grasp the faculties faster than the other two and surprisingly are gifted with wisdom to foretell the future. Perhaps mostly their insight is based on current events, and can also *feel* nature's vibes in the air to detect climatic change and crustal waves coming from the ground before a quake or a volcano erupts."

"Do you have any of them with you here?" David asked.

"Not here in this gathering, but there are a few with us on Urna."

"You mentioned they give birth, how do they conceive and deliver?" Fiona was eager to know.

"Nature has worked it out wonderfully for them, it is remarkable how they conceive. They are capable of self-impregnation by inner mechanism within their system. Delivery of a child is a unique process. Days before the baby is ready to emerge, the stomach begin to peal like a flower and when all the petals are in full bloom the baby comes out, shortly after, it retracts and heals in a few days. We respect them and hold them in high regard. Right now we have one just about ready to deliver in a few days, you are welcome to witness the event.

"Let me add, one of them foretold the catastrophe that would come to Sparka due to climatic change, the ice would melt and swallow the land; the reason for the hasty departure by my ancestor. The prediction was half correct, the water did rise. Sometime later while in space we got the news that the weather changed and the water did not do much damage. But in all fairness, he did sound an alarm much before the water began to rise, perhaps too early."

Ayond joined them, "You all seemed to be deeply engrossed in what he is telling you."

"It is so interesting to know that Zathenfur and his people live up to up fifteen hundred years that beats your span of life by about five hundred by your time scales." David said.

"To be honest I am confused by these numbers, let us think by our time scale on Urna." Fiona said.

"Now you can see the variety of life that exists in our galaxy. Perhaps there are countless others. Zathenfur added.

The party went on till hours.

Daniel and Fiona walked up to Ayond, "Dawn in an hour, have to take your leave." Bade goodbye to Ashtok and left. The rest began to follow, Ashtok was the last, he said, "Ayond you are always an excellent host, that's why we love to be in your home more often."

Daniel and Fiona reached home to find someone sitting at their door steps. The person stood up, and Daniel recognized him as one of Urna's elders with whom he often discussed the philosophy of life and the ultimate goal for achieving the limits to control the mind. His last meeting with him was some time ago, a meeting which he could remember up to that day.

Daniel's thoughts went back to some months ago when he visited the old man's house, the door was open, he entered, a loud voice greeted him but there was no one in the room. He stood puzzled, looked around and stepped outside but no trace of anyone. "I am behind you, I can see you but you can't see me." The voice said.

"No I can't unless I am blind. Where are you?"

'Now I am sure you can see me." The voice said as the old man materialised before him.

"Where have you come from appearing in front of me, this must be some kind of trick?"

"It is no trick, I have been standing next to you all along since you entered. Come inside I will tell you all about it."

They sat facing each other, his host began to fade away. Daniel just looked at the empty chair. Second later he reappeared.

"My good friend Daniel, remember once I told you that I was working on something very special; to achieve full control of the mind by tapping sections that give us dreams and extra sensory perceptions to be able to look in advance of events to take place in the future. Well, I finally achieved it. On your world few have attained it, the Tibetan monks for instance." Daniel's thoughts were interrupted by Fiona addressing the old man and escorting him into their house. "Have you been waiting long, please come inside?"

Fiona went to the kitchen and brought some refreshments and sat beside her husband.

"What brings you so early in the morning?"

"My good friend Daniel and Lady Fiona, what I am going to tell you must be kept in strict confidence. It is premature for anyone to know what I propose to do. Take a trip to the south where the primitive people of our kind live."

Daniel interrupted, "You should not, it is prohibited by the Supreme High to visit them."

"I fully realise the consequences, but I must."

"Why all of a sudden, what made you think or prompted you."

"You spoke the correct words, I did not think of them but they did."

"What do you mean, please don't talk in riddles."

Fiona was listening to the conversation curiously.

"Not riddles, they contacted me. Before you ask how, let me explain and do not interrupt. You know of my mental abilities, however, I have been receiving telepathic calls for help from an unknown source. Could not make out the language at first but then guessed that it is the one spoken by those people in the south. I am aware of the restrictions imposed by the authorities, it was on their request to be left alone and we in the north abided by it. Those people are like the ones who live in your Amazon forest, primitive and can be aggressive. I visited them long ago before the imposition of the ban, it was difficult in the beginning to learn what they liked and disliked, followed their rules and participated in their rituals, they worshiped a carved out giant block of rock as deity which had the resemblance to our Supreme High. They have never seen him, quite a coincidence.

"Perhaps ......" Fiona was about to say something when Daniel waved a hand not to interrupt.

The old man continued, "I asked them who that deity was? They said he descended from the sky, showed them how to grow better crops and share it with all, treated the sick, built better huts and advised them to give up fighting amongst themselves. I helped them in many ways and when decided to leave, they begged me to stay but I left with the promise to return. Now after many years they must be in need of my help. Must have performed rituals, genuinely concentrating in trances which must have stimulated their subconscious mind to transmit vibes which reached me during my meditative state. That is how I must have received those calls. It was not once but three times. I am compelled to go. Please keep it secret until I return."

"What about your other faculties ...." Before Daniel could finish his sentence, the old man raised his hand, "Now is not the time, all is in order, will talk about it after my return." With those words he left.

Daniel and Fiona sat thinking. He, about the higher mental level to communicate, the switch within to turn imperceptible and to what extent it would go. On the other hand she thought of the primitive tribe living as their ancestors did for eons, unchanged and needed help from a miracle man.

CHAPTER 20

The old man through a reliable contact of his own, managed a clandestine sojourn to the south. Early dawn, he disembarked miles out on the open and walked to where the natives lived. The place was empty, he sat below the engraved statue of their deity and dozed off to be awakened hours later by the commotion of the excited voices of the natives. The chief was called and he instantly recognised him. A ritual was performed to welcome him. When it was over, the old man asked the chief in their dialect, "You called me, I am here, what can I do for you?"

The chief humbly sauntered up to the idol, touched it and said loudly, "You have carried my message and he is here as I had requested you." He bowed and kissed it.

He turned to the old man, "You heard my call. We need your help, the good spirit has abandoned us, our crops are yielding less and many of our people are dying of starvation and sickness. You taught us how to ask for help and you are here to save our people." He said and touched the divine rock.

The old man gently replied, "I have no powers to help you but there is one who can. I can request him to come, but you have to listen to him very carefully and must accept his terms to make you a great tribe."

"We cannot accept anyone but the great one who visited us long ago," The chief said.

The old man had no idea who that statue represented, but the similarity gave him an idea.

"I can bring you a more powerful spirit who looks like this one," pointed at the idol, "He is much more powerful and can give you plenty of food."

The chief consulted with some of his men, they all hummed a prayer and the chief walked to the old man.

"We agree, bring him and if he is good we will remove the old one and make a new statue for him."

His mission was short, he made a phone call to his contact to take him back. On his return he called Daniel. They met, Daniel was amazed by his story but thought that it will go well with Ashtok who had forbidden any contact with the natives.

"Give me a few days and hopefully I will come with a positive answer."

Daniel had to think how to approach Ashtok who would be furious to learn about the old man's visit. He discussed the situation with David. Both decided to seek Ayond's advice.

"Ashtok will not be pleased as he had forbidden any interaction with the natives as they had demanded it and you say they came to him and asked for help..." David interrupted Ayond and said, "They did not physically come to him but contacted through some sort of telepathic message."

"That would make it more complicated, how could a primitive savage communicate telepathically…" Daniel interrupted her and explained, "Let me give you the background of the events leading to this story. The old man had visited and lived with those so called savages many years ago before the ban and they respect him. On the other hand he is very special, Ashtok will be pleased to learn of his mental ability to turn his body invisible. I have worked with him for many years and he has contributed a lot to the mental upgrading of the younger generation. He is an asset to Urna and its future. What if Ashtok makes a visit and helps them at the time of need. We may be looking at a new treaty to work together and perhaps make them part of the northern region."

"What did you mean by turning invisible? That is ludicrous for me to mention the word. How can such….."

"Ayond I have seen him do it, he is special."

"If you say so, but I have to be convinced first before I make a fool of myself."

A meeting was arranged at Daniel's home. David and Ayond sitting on the sofa, waited for the old man to show up. Impatiently Ayond remarked, "How long have we to wait before he shows up."

"On the contrary, he came in before you both arrived. You were late." Daniel said with a smile.

"Then where is he?" Ayond asked looking around.

"He is sitting on the sofa opposite you." Daniel said.

Ayond pointed to the empty sofa. "It is empty, can't see anyone but you standing next to it."

Just then, the old man's apparition began to form, with a broad smile he said, "Pleased that you could come."

Amazed, Ayond got up and nervously extended her hands to feel him. "He is real." She said tensely.

"Of course I am real, are you convinced?" he said softly.

"More than ever, I am sure Ashtok will be thrilled by your achievements and would gladly oblige you and offer to help those natives." She said.

It took Ayond courage to bring the subject to Ashtok. After some deliberations of how Daniel and his school is fairing to achieve mental supremacy in tapping unlocked doors within, "There is one man who has achieved the unthinkable."

"What do mean?" Ashtok asked.

"He can turn himself invisible, as we do with our aircrafts."

"How is it possible for a person of flesh and blood? I am a machine, can be performed on me like we do with our equipment, but can't be done on that kind of matter."

"Why not see it for yourself."

"Ayond, you are a scientist, it is some kind of a trick like magicians do."

"Why not see it for yourself and make up your mind?" She exclaimed hotly.

"If you insist, please bring him to me. I want Zathenfur and the others to witness it."

"If you are satisfied, please listen to what he has to say, and I expect you to agree. He has a proposal that would benefit the planet as a whole."

"You seem to be convinced, that is good enough for me. Your judgements have always been correct, but first as a formality must see this miracle performed. Such an accomplishment would be a step forward to the evolution of the body."

The old man along with Daniel and all the others arrived at Ashtok's residence. After an introduction by Daniel on the work they have been pursuing together, he turned to ask the old man to step forward and perform, but he was not to be seen anywhere in the room. There was a commotion and from a distance a voice cried, "Are you looking for me?"

They all stood quizzically searching for the source of the voice. Next to Ashtok an apparition began to materialise. It waved a hand, "Hello everyone," then faded. Ashtok moved his hands in the empty space where the old man stood moments ago. He reappeared again standing next to Daniel.

"Incredible, I have seen it and am convinced, what do you what from me?" Ashtok said condescendingly.

The old man explained in detail about the primitive tribe and also mentioned the look alike deity which they held in great esteem. Ashtok guessed it to be none other than the Guardian who must have visited them sometime in the past.

"I have always thought of those natives, wanted to help but left them alone as they were too entrenched in their beliefs and considered any changes as sacrilege. They had requested us to stay away and we abided by the commitment. If they are willing to accept our assistance we will give it on humanitarian grounds and if they are willing to merge with the rest of the inhabitants of this planet, meaning us in the north, will gladly accept them. Our entire planet is one large landmass, it would be good if all live as one." Ashtok said.

A few days later, Ashtok, Ayond and the old man arrived on the outskirts of the forest. The tribe who had not seen a flying ship land, came out and stood a few feet away from it. Bewildered and amazed waited in silence. A door slid open and a stairway sprawled from the craft. The first to disembark was the old man. The chief rushed to meet him. Next was Ayond, being a woman, she was greeted with a basket of fruit.

The climax was when Ashtok appeared at the doorway. There was a unanimous soft moans, the chief fell to the ground in prostration followed by the assembled tribe. The old man helped the chief up who was trembling all over. Ashtok descended and walked up to him and placed his hand on his shoulder, a tribal respect for an elder. The chief reciprocated, being just about five feet tall his hand could only reach up to the chest of the towering figure.

They entered the forest, and the chief said to the old man, "Is he the father of our deity who abandoned us. He looks like him but his shine is different"

Ayond saw the large rock sculptured with an effigy close in resemblance to Ashtok. She guessed the similarity and presumed the Guardian must have visited them.

The chief nervously pointed to the rock and asked Ashtok, "Are you his father?"

Unsure how to answer, he involuntarily answered, "Yes."

"Please send him back to us."

"He is travelling now, but will ask him to visit you when he is back."

"Must have gone to meet his family up there." The chief pointed to the sky.

Ashtok not wanting to go in detail said, "You will meet him soon, tell me how I can help you?" He patiently heard all their grievances and promised to send people from the north to help them grow better harvest, treat the sick, teach them the art of writing and introduce the use of modern tools. "All those people will help you, learn from them and treat them as you treat me and my son. They will also make a better statue of my son. You don't need one of mine."

The chief was pleased, performed a ritual ceremony and loudly proclaimed for all to hear, "The father of our god has assured us of everlasting happiness. Better food and no sickness, we shall learn new ways of the northern people and be part of them. Also we thank my old friend who brought the father of our deity and his wife."

Ayond wanted to correct that assumption but the old man whispered, "Let them think so, it makes no difference if they believe it or not."

Ayond humbly condescended.

On their way back to the north, Ashtok asked Ayond, "Do you know anything about the Guardian ever visiting them?"

"He never talked about the subject, must have landed there first before coming over to the north when we were still part of our binary system before we were jettisoned out. Our records show rather vaguely how he had materialised on Urna and met different levels of species on the planet. Perhaps he was referring to those natives and ourselves. He was then engrossed in developing our sciences and of course was responsible for bringing the master machine from the world he came from. That machine was you, a stationary cube then, but now thanks to him, you are made into an entity as we are." (xvi)

Ashtok recollected, "When he retrieved me from the world I was made on and took me to Urna and briefly narrated how he happened to be there, talked about the difference between the north and the south, one culturally ahead and the other far behind. I did not give much importance to that statement at the time. That was long ago, the important thing was his association with the natives leaving a good impression which is paying dividends now. I believe in the saying, 'the first impression is the last impression'. It surely applies to all walks of life.

"Coming back to the people of the south, we will stop referring to them as savages or the primitive tribe. Until we decide on an appropriate name, just refer to them as the people of the south. The old man will accompany our agricultural team, physicians and teachers and stay until they are well-adjusted. On his return a new school will be established for him to impart his knowledge with the assistance of Daniel and Fiona.

CHAPTER 21

Months had passed and work on Mars ran smoothly to Ashtok' satisfaction. "It is a matter of time before we hit the jack pot."

"I have noticed you are using words and phrases commonly used by us humans. You will really hit the jack pot when Mars starts to bloom." David said. Just then they were interrupted by a call from the Guardian.

"Some news leaked out, the Space Agency had secretly launched a probe some months ago heading for Ganymede, Jupiter's largest moon. It will pass close to Mars, plans to take photographs and before reaching Jupiter collect information on Urna. I was given this information secretly by a senior employee not pleased with their decision despite your earlier warnings to keep away from flying beyond the moon towards the Jovian planets. He resigned as a matter of principle and will be given a position in the New World Order."

"Leave it to me, I'll get back to you."

"I suspect it is not Ganymede they are aiming at, it is Mars and Urna. They are itching to know what is going on, especially after their astronauts' encounter. Ashtok appraised the Urna Administrative Council headed by Ayond.

195

"I have a strong suspicion, astronomers on Earth are not going to let go their probing easily. After our bumping with those astronauts they genuinely believe in the existence of some sort of life besides our own. I am sure they have not disclosed it to the world, want to be the first ones to make contact. They may have even guessed that we are somewhat involved. The probe is due soon, surely will survey Mars and Urna. As it is unmanned we can just redirect it back to them after erasing all its functions. They will get back a lump of dumb metal, with a simple message, *'we told you so'* those four words say it clearly that we are in control." Ashtok concluded.

A team of experts flew out to meet the approaching probe, electronically erased all its functional data, leaving it empty, a dumb ball of metal and put in new commands to orbit Mars and sling shot its way back home. The probe followed those directives and merrily changed course, along with those four words.

In a matter of hours the Space Agency began to receive the message from the probe. Scornfully they were furious but could do nothing. News leaked out and the headline boldly said, *'We Told You So! A Message from Mars'*. The next line read, *'Space is out of bounds for Earth'*. The Guardian conveyed the news to Ashtok and also an interesting piece of information. His intelligence department intercepted a communique about a secret meeting in an obscure location between the presidents of the United States and the Russian Federation. "It would be impossible for me to know its purpose."

"Keep me informed if you hear anything. Do not interfere in any way," Ashtok ordered.

Ten days later the Guardian received an unexpected invitation from the President of the United States of America.

On arrival at the White House, he was warmly greeted and taken to the Oval Office. To his surprise he saw the Russian President seated comfortably and two other gentlemen whom he did not recognise.

The American President shook hands and seated him next to the Russian. Then introduced the other two, an American and a Russian, the heads of two special departments created to handle the affairs of a secret understanding between the two super powers in line with the New World Order. He sat down and said to the Guardian. "These two minds," pointing to the Russian and himself, "Had been working on this for some time. Studied its pros and cons and came out with one question. What are we bickering about, when we have a beautiful world to live on and are alive to enjoy it. The bottom line of all our problems is a kind of intolerance of ideologies and cultures, innate in most of us. We must do away with it, archaic dogmas to divide the world into segments, tribal in nature. On both sides we have established men and women who understand our venture. We shook hands on it and now we are ready to serve mankind.

"Our prime targets would be to eradicate terrorism in all forms, the causes that prompt them and genuinely make this planet, our home, a safe place to live. We shall police the world to maintain good behaviour, impart justice impartially, no favouritism and help in eliminating poverty and sickness as far as possible. With this understanding the NWO or the New World Order will achieve its objectives. It was after seeing the television broadcast in which the immense power was display by the one who called himself the Supreme High who is your boss, we came to believe in the genuine determination of the alien's true intentions to make this world a better place; out of love for the human race and their ecstatic abode called Earth. With due respect to you and the Supreme High not being human, but an artificial entity, we have great respect and admiration for what you are trying to achieve which we humans have failed or even realised its genuine resolve. To strengthen your efforts we will act discreetly as the keepers of law and order with your full knowledge but will not announce it to the world yet. With our success sanity will prevail, at the same time will send a message to conniving politicians and political fencing of the old days will become a thing of the past. We sent feelers to some trusted allies, all were in favour." He concluded.

The Russian reaffirmed his support and added, "Most turmoil between nations are aided and in some cases fueled by big powers. To some extent we are responsible for the chaos we are in, with the absence of big muscles calm will gradually follow. This is our chance to prove our good intention to ease your expectations for peaceful existence. We will jointly outdo all forms of terrorism, wherever and whoever is responsible."

The Guardian thanked both presidents for their concern and magnanimous efforts and added, "My Supreme High, the boss, would surely welcome your good intentions. I will convey to him. Meanwhile, go ahead with your plans, should you require any assistance from me, just ask and I shall provide."

As soon as he left conveyed to Ashtok, "Those two great nations have come with an unprecedented handshake and understand the meaning of peace, the rest of the world will greatly benefit and it will paves the way to the fruition of our objectives." Ashtok was pleased and gave his approval.

During the next three months the Americans and the Russians met, named their joint operation *The Flying Doves* and made a list of priority trouble spots. The first on the list was the Middle East, where five sovereign nations were fighting insurgencies who surfaced against legitimate governments and indiscriminately massacring innocent lives. For decades the atrocities continued, civilians uprooted from their homes living in shelters or exiled as refugees as their cities were reduced to rubble.

The second was to solve a chronic problem between a handful of nations who traditionally quarrelled on ideological and cultural ethnicity, in some cases caused conflicts, supported by major powers for political gains. Other troubled areas were localised within their territorial borders.

In a joint and unprecedented announcement the two super powers declared to the world the formation of *The Flying Doves* to monitor and maintain law and order. Their task will be to eradicate international crimes, such as those encroaching on legitimate nations and on those who propagate their ideological and cultural doctrines and impose it forcibly. They will also help to normalise dis-satisfied forces that exist within nations.

The world was stunned by the declaration and some suspiciously viewed it as a conspiracy to dominate the world and regarded it as a faction of The New World Order.

The Flying Doves approached the insurgents in the Middle East and asked them to give up their unlawful intrusions civilly, it was rejected. They preferred to continue their belligerent plight.

The Flying Doves had no option but to end the rebellions vehemently. Their secret operatives located and placed electronic devices to indicate the location of military installations, ammunition warehouses and pockets of insurgent units spread across the five nations which they have forcibly occupied.

The Flying Doves were ready to strike. On a Friday at two in the morning air crafts flew in from the north of the troubled territory and scrambled westwards, at the same time a similar squadron entered from the south and flew eastwards. The electronic devises pin pointed the targeted location and the fighter jets let loose their deadly assault. For miles, east and west, north and south the night was filled with flaming pockets of burning remains. The onslaught lasted for days. Soon after, thousands of airborne paratroopers descend onto the targeted area. They were spotted, from the ground they were targeted like pigeons but most who made it turned hundreds of miles into a battleground filled with the sounds of crackling machine guns and exploding bombs. Pillars of dark smoke rose high from different pockets of the battle zones, in days accumulated and formed a gloomy canopy above the entire area. Nights lit by burning vehicles and equipment. The combat was bloody and merciless with heavy losses on both sides. Finally in the fifth week the transgressors were eliminated. The entire area from east to west was littered with thousands of corpses, smouldering vehicles, artillery and equipment.

A formal announcement was made, '*The Flying Doves* have achieved in just over a month what others with joined forces of several countries could not accomplish in years. They are here to serve all peace loving nations.' No sooner the announcement was made, an African, a South America and two Asian nations sought their help. In a matter of days the rioters were quelled in all four locations.

But all was not over, for some conniving terrorist leaders the war may be over temporally but their battles for achieving what they had started continued. An unknown television station calling itself the 'Free Voice of Liberty' announced that the so called *The Flying Doves* days are numbered and soon they will be grounded. It also stated that the war which according to them has been won is not yet over. It will soon spread like wild fire and consume those who support the self-proclaimed policing force. In response to that challenge *The Flying Doves* set its intelligence services to root out the ring leaders of the clandestine broadcast. It did not lake long, monetary rather than other means speeded the unveiling of a large international network of operatives supported by well-armed militia in a number of countries. With the help of local support the stage was set for The Flying Doves to make their move. Late one night, simultaneously in all the suspect locations the ring leaders and most of their mercenaries were rounded up. In some instances brief exchange of artillery ensued but were eliminated or made to surrender. They were no match for a well-equipped force. The prisoners were paraded in their local sports stadiums and summarily executed. An announcement offered to dissidents who were on the loose to submit within seventy two hours and face a jail sentence with the proviso for early release on good behaviour, failing which, if caught would be executed.

Many came forward, on goodwill they were sentenced to five years. With that the world was free from trouble makers, or appeared so. Two south Asian nations were on the verge of a bloody confrontation, *The Flying Doves* flew in and talked to each government. They were told, in the event of war both will lose their status as independent nations and will be taken over by the New World Order. With that warning both submitted and peace was restored. Some trouble spots existed worldwide, but were different in nature. Local dissidents against their governments' policies. No action was taken as they were internal matters, only cautionary advice was given to the authorities to solve the grievances peaceably.

The Guardian announced the successes of *The Flying Doves,* "They have removed the bad elements from the midst of peace loving people. Let me request you, not to indulge on anything contrary to the interest of the community that may bring unnecessary pain and sorrow." Despite the warning there were still some disgruntled nations bound by cultural traditions and were not convinced by the intentions of the New World Order, only out of fear they towed the line.

Within a year the slate was clean from nations interfering with the affairs of others. Only within the borders of some religious prosecutions and unjust subjugations existed, which have always been there. A warning was issued.

On hearing the news of stability, Ashtok was happy and send messages of congratulations to the presidents of the United States and Russia, with a post script, 'Keep the Doves Flying High.'

In response they sent a reply back, "To the Supreme High Mr. Ashtok, we have now understood the power of unity, the world will be safe and the New World Order shall succeed in its endeavours. We thank you and the people of Urna for their valued help to enlighten and guide us with the truth and shall always continue to shine with eternal hope and prosperity."

CHAPTER 22

Three years had passed and the functioning of the New World Order had achieved its goals. Only seven nations had abstained from joining it, the reason they had given was, it does not conform to their cultural values and religious beliefs. They were rich due to the abundance of mineral resources, did not have the foresight to foresee the repercussions that followed. Non-member countries were not entitled to have ambassadorial representation, trading rights, financial or any other assistance and were treated as nonexistent. Soon their egoistic lofty heads began to stoop and the seclusion from the fraternity was felt. Food became scarce, sickness and disease eroded the population, they were left to feel the pinch. The world watched with pity, their hands were tied to help. Some of their leaders approached the New World Order for membership but were denied. Again pleaded, and were told to relinquish their leaderships and handover the reigns of administered to the New World Order. Those countries were on the verge of a civil war and fearing the repercussions, they humbly complied. *The Flying Doves* were given the task to handle the situation.

Ashtok had no more worries regarding Earth, *The Flying Doves* had paved the way for the smooth running of the world organization. He concentrated on developing Mars and announced to the members of the Urna Administrative Council, "The acclimatisation process of the weather is proceeding most satisfactorily with the dark energy power source provided by Zathenfur."

"Have there been any signs on the instruments to indicate that?" Someone asked.

"Not from the instruments, the Marants have told me so."

"What makes them so sure?"

"When I asked the same question, they said '*could feel the smell.*'"

"What does that mean, did they explain how?"

"Yes, through their skin and nose, an ability which humans and our people do not possess. However, I would still depend on our instruments but do not entirely dismiss their sense to feel the change, after all they evolved there and may have developed traits that sound farfetched to us. Zathenfur is considering to place the dark energy batteries on the two moons of Mars that would neutralise the radiation level. That energy has some strange abilities, deployed well by those who understand its uncanny infrastructure can do the impossible. They harnessed that energy for thousands of years and can apply it to suite any situation, we are fortunate to have him and his people.

"In a few days, I will be inspecting the final touches to our first domed city on Mars which I have named *Ayond,* the person whose name it bears has served our people with love and care; she is like a mother to them."

The day arrived when senior members of the Council, Ayond, David, Sam and his wife Aishtra the Jinn, Jim and his wife, Daniel and his wife Fiona, Saeed the Egyptian, Zathenfur and some of his colleagues all boarded *The Gentle Stream*.

Seeing them seated, Ashtok before going to the controls looked at his passengers and said, "What a collection of jewels I have here, you all sparkle like precious stones. You will do me the honour to be the first to step into the first city on a planet long uninhabited. In days to come more will be built and filled with people. Today we are on an inspection tour, workers and technicians will still be around but they will not bother us."

Being on *The Gentle Stream* was like being onboard a cruise liner, entertainment, lavish cuisines and views on the outside from large windows displayed infinite number of stars that whizzed by, kept them diverted from their long journey. On arrival they were greeted by a lifeless hazy barren sphere. After orbiting the planet, the ship descended near the only structure with some vehicles standing by.

Before disembarking all put on the skin tight fit suits and facial masks, except Ashtok and Aishtra being a Jinn. At the main entrance of the city they entered a room and waited. The gate shut behind them and the room began to fill with breathable air, moments later they entered the city. "Now you can remove your masks." They were told. They were greeted by the Marants Elders who had arrived earlier.

"It will not be very long when all of you can step out of the dome without the need to wear those cumbersome masks." Ashtok said.

"What a relief it will be, may not live long enough to enjoy it but future generations will." David remarked.

"What a wonderful new world it will be, just as it was once before. Our only fear is the presence of humans, Ashtok has promised to bring good people like our earth friends who are with us here." A Marants Elder commented.

"That is my pledge." Ashtok replied.

"We trust your judgement."

The chief technician working at the site led the visitors on a tour. He began, "The dome height at its centre is one hundred and fifty feet. The material the dome is made of is a kind of transparent metal stronger than steel and its thickness is six feet, comprised of six layers, each one is a foot thick."

"Excuse me, if the source of the material is metallic, how is it transparent?" Sam asked.

"It is not a metallic metal but from a substance which has stronger qualities than a metal, similar to plastic that is why it is transparent, besides it has another quality, it can heal itself if cracked or broken by a meteorite. Such an elements is unknown to humans but will not be long before discovering it. You have some brilliant minds in your world."

They moved towards the wall, David touched it and said, "I can see through it with ease, can't be six feet thick."

"That is the beauty of this material, you can put a dozen sheets and visibility would be the same as a single sheet. The dome is strong enough to resist strong winds, radiation surges and small meteorites."

They moved around the parameter, gardens with green fresh grass, sprouting plants and a few benches to sit on. They entered the building and were shown an apartment. The technician explained, "These are for human type living and on the other side of the building are accommodations for our hosts, the Martians or the Marants. They have it a bit different and have requested me not to show it as their living style is of different configurations. Perhaps someday they will invite you. On this side we have something they do not have, and they don't need it, a swimming pool. Water is piped from the underground lakes." From the basement they entered a long dark passage, "This tunnel goes deep inside for shelter in case of an emergency, it is not yet complete and our tour ends here."

On their return journey David put a question to Ashtok, "The whole complex is very impressive like living in a normal environment, but there is always the danger of large meteorites or asteroid, the tunnel would not be safe enough."

"We will have ships stationed equipped with the same magnetic repellent force you witness on this ship *The Gentle Stream,* when we encountered an asteroid on our inaugural flight. They can deal with such a threat."

Back on Urna, Ashtok called the Guardian and enquired about his progress in the selection of immigrants to Mars.

"I could only select thirty seven willing young families with two children each, that makes a total of hundred and eleven." The Guardian said.

"A good number, start with their medicals and drills needed for space travel. Their luggage should be minimal, they may carry photos, pets like cats, dogs and birds. I will send you a list of animals, a separate ship will carry them."

CHAPTER 23

· · · · · · · · ● ● ● ● ● ● ○○○○○○○ · · ·

At the main underground weather control centre on Mars, the head supervisor in-charge walked around checking readings on instruments and equipment related to the acclimatisation of the planet. On a wall a large five feet wide barometer, with numerous little windows within it displayed readings with pin lights of different colours, each indicating the climatic infrastructure on the outside. After completing his round he comfortably settled on a reclining chair and was soon deeply engrossed reading a book. It was late at night, his ears picked a brief sharp and loud buzzing sound, thinking it to be a fly or a mosquito his reflexes involuntarily moved a hand to whisk it away. Moments later the buzz came back, he was irritated, with the book he lashed hard grazing his ear. "Damn it, I must have hit it." Started reading, suddenly he stopped, put the book down and jumped out of his chair, "What I am saying, no damned mosquitoes or flies on Mars, what was it?"

The buzz came again. He looked around trying to trace the source. His eyes caught a riffle of green light on one of the little windows on the large circular dial. He stared at it, and the flicker came back again, lasted for a fraction of a second. He knew what it meant. Let a wide grin across his face. "Take your time, I am in no hurry." He said and settled back on his reclining chair, opened his book and started to read. The pages appeared blank as his thoughts were elsewhere. "The barometer is trying to tell me something." He said to himself, threw the book and walked up to it. "It can't be a glitch. It happened before but there was no green light, it must be the real thing." Just then the buzzing came louder and the light flickered longer. Staring at the large dial with his eyes fixed indefinitely, to his joy he noticed a slight vibration of the large needle. He guessed what it meant. Relaxed, he poured himself a cup of coffee, sipped leisurely with eyes pinned to the barometer. A little later decided to check the outside, switched the survey monitor, there was no indication of any thing extraordinary. He was tired and exhausted, decided to sleep and make a complete check in the morning. "Perhaps a false alarm, an anomaly in the mechanism." He thought.

He couldn't get a long sleep, woke up and to his amazement saw the green light was on, not blinking and the needle had shifted slightly. He switched on his survey monitor to look outside. Nothing extraordinary, looked the same as always. He called some of his colleagues to double check, they confirmed all the electronic devices were in order and his observation of the barometer reading did indicate a change in the elements on the outside. They put on their suits and went to the top. No visible signs, but the manual reader showed what the instrument below had indicated.

Several days later, just before dawn the supervisor was awakened by one of his assistants, "Been on the top, saw something in the distance, like a misty film." He said excitedly.

Quickly they rushed up, the sun was making its entrance, far above them a thin layer of gilded hazy formation gently drifted eastwards.

They were joined by other members of the team and watched the phenomena. They went back to the control room and the instruments showed a change from the usual weather pattern. Hours later they went up again, the mist had disappeared. "The heat of the sun must have dissipated it." Someone said.

The instruments continued to show positive results. For several days they observed the formation of the hazy mist that starts late at night and lasts till mid mornings. The supervisor checked with all other locations where the Oxygenators were located. It was happening mostly in the southern hemisphere. He reported to Ashtok. His instructions were to keep him informed on daily bases.

Three months had passed without a significant change but the instruments continued to register positive results. The supervisor made it a habit to step on to the top before dawn and waited until the sun came up. Weeks past with the same drill, at times he was accompanied by a colleague or two. Not long after, one morning they were greeted by patches that looked like clouds, sprinkled randomly, last for an hour then dissolute into fragments by the wind. It was conveyed to Urna, the news spread and there were jubilations.

Month after month cloud formations were becoming more promising mainly in the southern hemisphere of the planet. The climate was adjusting its pattern depending on temperature variations. Ashtok was overjoyed when he was informed that for several days cloud formations were thickening and stayed longer. For Ashtok it was time to visit. He informed the Marants Elders of his proposed visit.

The Gentle Stream landed with Ayond, Zathenfur and their colleagues. The city was different from their last visit. The garden was in full bloom, plants had budded with flowers. After a brief tour they settled down in the apartments in the complex. They were told by Ashtok, "This will be your home until Mars showers its welcome." During the day they routinely enjoyed the facility as being on an exotic vacation. A favourite spot was the swimming pool and sauna, with an indoor cafeteria and a mini pub. The movie theater and a small library of books were an added attraction. Just before sunset the dome's open space was lit, and the residents emerged, strolled, and sat in groups, meals were served in the open. On the outside was darkness all around, the only interest was watching the glimmer of the night sky dotted with countless stars when not obstructed by any cloud. The same routine day in and day out. The Marants Elders visited regularly. Days passed and to their disappointment there was no significant indication of change in the weather pattern. Cloud formation continued to take different shapes and thickness, occasionally lingered longer, but often just a thin layer and dissipate by late afternoons. The daily report continued to show positive changes. "We have to be patient and wait. Weather is unpredictable, we have no choice but to stay as long as it takes, don't want to miss the first spark that will ignite life on Mars." Ashtok said stubbornly.

On the fifth week, around midday the sun began to lose it brightness by a film of grayish vapour approaching from the west. Electric lights in the dome began to gradually compensate for the loss of brightness. That scenario remained unchanged for several days and they waited expectantly. One late afternoon their hopes were rekindled, a thin grayish vapour began to thicken, churned and swirled. For a long time they looked up for a possible sign of it turning into a bank of clouds and perhaps see a flicker of lightening, but the sky remained the same, dull and suspenseful. Not wanting to miss that chance, it was decided that one of them would keep a two hourly night watch. For two days nothing dramatic, but on the third day, late afternoon the swirling thickened turned into thick dark agitating clouds. All pinned against the transparent wall and stared up in awe for the moment they had been waiting for; a marvel which would herald its entrance.

Ashtok gladly announced, "Ladies and gentlemen, the moment has arrived, at any moment now we hopefully will be witnessing a miracle aided by technology. Our machines which had been processing water vapour from the underground lakes is about to pay dividend. Tonight no one shall sleep until you are completely drenched, not literary but metaphorically. He requested Aishtra and Fiona to make arrangements for drinks and meals to celebrate the impending change to a sterile world.

The Marants Elders arrived minutes after the party had begun. Music echoed, drinks flowed and the dance floor vibrated. The sun was just above the horizon occasionally obstructed by a hazy layer of mist. The festivity began to warm up, the music filled the air and the floor echoed by the rigors of dancing feet. One of the Elders asked Ashtok, "Never seen such behaviour, do humans react so acrobatically by twisting their body frame when they hear music?"

"Not always, but often on happy occasions."

"Does this mean they are not happy all the time?"

"Not really, ask your teachers, they can explain it to you better." He did not want to elaborate more.

An Elder turned to his colleague, "Make a note, we had no idea, our teachers could explain."

Meanwhile, the clouds twisted and churned, all the chemical ingredients were being administered as in a laboratory, waiting for a consequence. It happened all of a sudden. A blinding bright flash of light lit miles of terrain, within the dome the luminosity was brighter than a sunny day and before anyone could react an ear-piercing loud thunderous blast followed. All within the dome froze-still where they stood. Silently they paced towards the wall to look outside, leaned their heads against it and cupped their hands around their foreheads and peered. It was dark, they waited for an encore, but there was no apparent activity in the clouds, silence had filled the air.

Sam walked up to Ashtok, "That was the brightest lightning strike I have seen and the loudest sound that followed. How did we hear it so loud inside?"

"We have outdoor sensors attached to the dome. You may continue with what you are doing until the next firework display. The party atmosphere sobered and the music of Albinoni and Pachelbel in the background softly filled the air.

Ashtok stood alone. "I can imagine future cities like this one with happy people." He mused.

After dinner they grouped and chatted but kept vigilance for more heavenly fireworks.

Zathenfur walked up to Ashtok, "The dark energy power has not only made your machines more efficient but also helped stabilize the elements. Its mysterious effects are mind boggling and has many enigmatic behaviours in shaping the clock-work of the cosmos."

"To which not only I but the people of Urna join me to thank you for the gift of the energy source, with it we will achieve more wonders."

Someone shouted, "I see some faint flashes of lightning."

The entire entourage scrambled towards the glassy wall. Before reaching it, a massive lightning bolt with horrendous streaks of intricate shapes and sizes snaked down and around the dome, complimented by ear-piercing crashing and roaring thunder strikes. Successive and uninterrupted firework display seemed unending, after several minutes all went quiet. There was a lull. All waited sombrely for the show to make another dramatic exhibit. Only faint and defused flashes crept across the dark canopy. After a while all except Fiona, dispersed. She was deeply absorbed and stayed pinned to the wall. Her eyes caught a droplet meander down in front of her, she was unsure, looked up at the diffused flashes, more droplets trickled down and meandered along the wall, obstructing her view. Impulsively she let a scream so loud that echoed within the dome. "We have raiiiin!" No sooner the echo subsided, a brilliant bolt of lightning flashed followed by a loud crashing burst of thunder. She shouted again hysterically, "Thank you Vulcan, some more please!"

Before anyone could react, successive and seemed unending more flashes and deafening bursts of thunder boomed from all directions, all of sudden a heavy down pour, cascading endlessly beating against the dome, scattering gravel off the ground and no sooner was absorbed by the thirsty soil.

Ayond and David walked up to Sam who was talking with Aishtra and Daniel. There was a naughty smirk on their faces, pointed to the outside, "How about it chaps, ready for a dip!" Ayond said impishly.

"Do you mean it, lead on, we are behind you." Sam said.

"Wait here, let me get the boss's approval."

Ashtok was reluctant at first, seeing Ayond's disappointed face, gave his consent. "It is risky with those lightning strikes, but if you must, don't say long, put on your masks and take a couple of security men just in case."

Outside, the down pour was heavy, like a stream from a water fall. They formed a circle and merrily jumped up and down raising their hands and began to chant familiar songs. Inside the dome the rest watched and some began to mimic them. The jubilation was infectious, Ashtok involuntarily tiptoed and mingled with them.

The Marants Elders looked on and exchanged curious glances. They walked up to Zathenfur and politely asked, "Do humans do this when water falls from the sky? Does falling water bring them to a mental imbalances?"

"Not so, they are just happy. People have many unusual ways to express joy." He explained.

"What about Ashtok, he is not human?"

"He too, is perhaps in a joyous mood."

The Elders gathered, one of them said, "Strange habits, they wriggled like crazy with music and now jump up and down when water falls from above. We have to make a curious study, make a note. It will help us to understand a little more about the human behaviour. It has infected the Supreme High, soon we may get that urge."

Shortly after, Ayond and her companions returned, changed their clothing and joined the rest. Ashtok asked his chief engineer to check on other location on the planet. He reported that it was mostly in the southern hemisphere, not so in the north.

Proudly Ashtok announced, "We have succeeded, Mars has woken up from its slumber, now it is our turn to make it stay that way."

For seven days it poured endlessly, filled gullies, washed mountain and hill sides. Formed pools and streams that zig zagged aimlessly but soon absorbed by the thirsty ground. Some pockets of puddles and wet patches changed the shape of the topography. The sun came out with specks of clouds that dotted the blue sky. The reddish haze of the Red Planet fading away.

They bade farewell to the Marants Elders and took off. From above they could see a few streams reflecting the sun light as in a dance of joy merrily flowing to unknown destinations. "The barren terrains will soon quench its thirst, in time after having its fill, the waters will stay to form pools and lakes, perhaps oceans sometime in the future." Ashtok commented.

"It just needed for someone to play a tune to wake it up." Aishtra put in.

When the two Martian moons came to view, Zathenfur said, "I have plans to install the dark energy packs on both to help stabilize the rudiments to keep Mars free from hazardous elements. You all have no idea what that power can do. Thousands of years ago when we lived in the Orion star system, we harnessed it and made it serve us faithfully in all walks of life that is why we call it *neumarak,* which means a life giver."

Ashtok was listening attentively and made a remark, "Which also means that your race is far older and more advanced in the sciences than the people who made me. I thought we had reached the zenith, which also mean the complexity of life that exists, perhaps there are much older civilizations than yours."

Zathenfur had to carefully word his reply, "Ashtok, pardon my saying, you are an all knowing machine, made by a highly intelligent race who put their wisdom in you, but the knowledge we inherited goes far beyond yours and we are not machines. What if there are others far superior to us and machines far more advanced than you."

"Very wisely put Zathenfur, the universe as we know it is billions of years old and the possibilities are limitless. Come to think of it, the humans on Earth are barely a few thousand years old, infants in that time scale, and hypocritically consider themselves as the masters of all they survey. It will be a very long time for them to realise the truth."

Back on Urna, Ashtok reported to the Administrative Council, "My job after so many years have succeeded, Mars has been awakened. Thanks for the assistance Zathenfur has provided us without which it would have taken longer. Once the dormant bacteria and the planting of seeds take root, the rest would be left to nature to do its part. Of course this will not happen overnight, but in the not distant future, some of you will be there to witness it." He added.

"What is your programme for bringing humans, we feel they will spread chaos and bring along their antiquated ideas?" Someone in the Council asked.

"The Guardian has made the selection and I trust his judgement, he will pick the best of the best to fulfill our requirement. Be rest assured."

"Any more questions?" Ashtok said.

Ayond being the head of the Council stood up and confidently assured the gathering, "The Supreme High Ashtok has spoken and his word is final. He has never failed us and it is because of his leadership and wisdom we are what we are today. Don't forget that."

CHAPTER 24

Mars was reborn and in its infancy, needed loving care and guidance which was provided. Ashtok was free and wanted to close the chapter with earth, free the Guardian and handover the responsibility to humans, but before that, he wanted to address the world body with all heads of states attending, no ambassadorial or any other person representing, unless incapacitated or seriously unwell. The Guardian sent invitations.

Ashtok and Ayond arrived and drove straight to the New World Order building. The Guardian escorted them to the assembly hall, all the members stood and applauded.

One of the Arab delegate whispered to the other, "He looks like the Guardian but his shine is like gold. If he is made of gold must worth a fortune."

"How I would like to melt him down, that gold will be in millions," His companion said with a bit of a laugh.

"Jokes aside, he and the Guardian resemble each other, must be from the same mother,"

"Come to think of it, both of them are androids and we humans are ruled by machines, what the world has come to?"

Before his companion could reply they were interrupted by the Guardian's opening address.

"Ladies and gentlemen, none of you has met our Supreme High Ashtok in person, you may have seen him on the television broadcast some time ago when he addressed you and displayed his powers on an empty desert landscape. He is here today to give you a simple advice and it will be his last. Those who do not heed to what he would request of you, would feel his wrath. He does not need your wealth or sympathy, for he has worlds under his command. Listen to him carefully, after he has finished you may freely ask any questions. I repeat, this is your last chance to clarify any doubts in your minds and remember he is the highest authority, above all your kings, presidents and heads of government.

"Also with us, is Madam Ayond, some may remember her? She was our head for many years when our people lived here. She is the second in command after our Supreme High.

He paused for a full minute, walked up to Ashtok and escorted him to the rostrum. "Ladies and gentlemen I present you Ashtok, the Supreme High of this world and many others.

Ashtok faced the audience, studied their faces and began. "Thank you all for attending." After a long pause, "First I want to put you at ease, I nor the Guardian are made of flesh and blood, in your terminology we are machines or androids but far superior than you can comprehend. We have the ability, if we wish to do something it can be done by the snap of our fingers, so to speak. Ayond on the other hand is a human form and is my assistant."

The two Arabs looked at each other and exchanged a few words, "He must have heard us or read our minds!"

The other just looked and nodded.

Ashtok continued, "Being what I am have no gray areas, with me it is either black or white. So you have to listen carefully and digest every word I say. There will be no buts or whys. What I say must be taken seriously. The days of ifs and buts are over. Comply or you are out of the New World Order. When that happens you will become nobody and will be ignored as an entity. You will starve and will be reduced to humiliating degradation, no one will come to your rescue. You will in no time vanish from this beautiful planet.

"The Americans and the Russians have come to an unprecedented handshake which has brought sanity to the world politics. Cleared cancerous elements that had plagued humanity, deep rooted in cultures worldwide for over two millenniums. Read your history books. The alliance of these two great nations has formed *The Flying Doves,* whose job will be to police and get rid of international crimes whatever their causes might be and prevent any unjust treatment of helpless citizens within your borders whether religious or political.

"Throughout history, millions have suffered by the hands who preached their faiths, butchered innocent natives of the Americas, not to mention the atrocities committed in Europe, Africa and Asia. For thousands of years, religious conquests and subjugation upon the weak and helpless. Ask yourselves why? You know the answer but dare not admit its hidden agenda. I can name a few, greed for wealth, agricultural properties, enslaving men for labour, women for pleasures and domestic chores, and of course converting nations forcefully and rule over them for political gains and supremacy. Who are you to judge who is right or who is wrong to believe in your gods? In the end why not leave it to your god to judge, reward or punish the offenders. In a nut shell, most of world issues are in some ways are a conflict of one belief against another. Spend your time more positively in improving the environment.

"I am not blaming anyone right now, you have inherited that modus operandi from your ancestors from time immemorial. In this modern age of technological advancement there are some who prefer the old ways and practice them discretely. I have nothing against religions or what you believe in, they are meant to make you good and better if followed correctly without hidden malice towards others. Do not make it a tool for personal gains.

"Based on what I have said, I decree the following proposals which are not negotiable and will remain in force for fifty years. I am a machine but do have some of humanity in me. After this meeting, you will be provided with a copy of this deliberation, study it very carefully and treat it as your guideline to run your lives in peace and harmony.

"All rituals of any religions and faiths of any nature, when conducted in places of worship, avoid any non-complimentary and slandering references to other beliefs. Such gatherings have become a platform for political or religious gains, a place for unnecessary blabbing. Strictly speaking worship is a private thing between yourselves and your creator. Nothing better if performed in the privacy of your homes. Gathering are merely a show and a display of presence, unless it is conducted in proper dignified manner and without distractions.

"The next point is an important rule, no one is to impose or cause harm to anyone of different faith within your boarders or in any way influence other nations. Anyone breaking the rule will cause to forfeit the entire community to continue the practice of that faith. The places of worship will be closed indefinitely whether in a village, a town or the entire nation depending on the circumstances.

"I do not want to hurt your feelings, give it a serious thought and you will realise I am right, the world will be a better place to live in. If you follow as I have instructed, the rules will be relaxed. There are billions of lives, each pursuing a goal, let everyone enjoy it, live and let live.

"I have decided to withdraw all my staff from your world and give you the opportunity to handle your affairs. The Guardian will relinquish his position. It will be filled only by one of the five permanent members for a period of ten years. The position as head of the New World Order can be held only by one of those members by rotation, assisted by the nine executive members, who are selected by rotation from the world body members for a similar period. *The Flying Doves* however, will act as a sentry, defaulters will be warned, if repeated appropriate punishment will be administered. I am also watching over them to perform justly. In brief, be good citizens on this wonderful planet. That is all I have to say, if you have any questions, feel free to ask." Ashtok concluded.

There was a passive half-hearted applause.

Ashtok waited.

Silence filled the hall, no one spoke. He knew his message had sunk in. There was no purpose for anyone to argue or make an observation, the rules were given and must be obeyed.

He walked out with the Guardian and Ayond, "I can feel they were not happy with what I have said and they know well that I will be watching and dare not disobey. All said and done, my inner thought is that it's a hopeless case. Some of them are as good as not being there, it has gone on deaf ears. Knowing their traits, they will certainly try to manipulate and undermine the system." Ashtok said.

"That challenge will not be difficult for *The Flying Doves* to handle unless the whole world turns insane." Ayond put in.

"It is no more our problem, but I can predict, a day will come when the world will turn crazy as Ayond said." The Guardian assumed.

Before leaving for Urna, he instructed the Guardian to finalise the selection of families to be moved to Mars, "Keep them in a ready state, physically and mentally. Can't give you a time frame right now will depends on the completion of the domed cities which may take some time. By the way, beside the list of animal that I will send you, please include a variety of butterflies, bees and some others insects, I leave it to your choice but no mosquitoes and flies."

On the ship, Ayond put a question. "What if anyone dared to disobey, you know how some manipulate the rules and always get away with it. You were not serious about......?"

Ashtok cut in, "More serious than ever before, if *The Flying Doves* fail in their mission, I will come down so hard on the one who breaks the rule and there will be no turning back. It will be exemplary to others. Basically human nature is good, but their weak points easily influence to go astray, depending on many factors and the culture they were brought up in. But that will change if the New World Order does its job properly. For now Earth is out of my mind, it is Mars I will concentrate on. The Guardian have managed thirty seven families with their children, a total of one hundred and eleven. Zathenfur and his people will also have their city, perhaps they will call it New Atlantis or Atland."

"You are forgetting Aishtra's species."

"They too will have theirs. I will be so happy the day all of them live on that new world and are called Martians."

CHAPTER 25

Besides the first domed city named *Ayond*, four more were completed, each four levels high. Occupants were sent for a short period on experimental basis. In one, families from Urna followed by some of Zathenfur's people. The third for the Marants, which was built close to their underground habitat, connected by tunnels for free access to move around and get familiar with the change in living. One was left for the earth immigrants. The capital city *Ayond*, was kept for Ashtok and his retinue, the Guardian, Ayond and her colleagues. Plans for future cities were demarcated close to where underground water was available.

While on Earth nations behaved and functioned as envisioned by the New World Order, the Guardian spent his time disposing some of his responsibilities for the ultimate handover of his functions to one of the permanent members as directed by the constitution of the world body. He sat with all the five permanent members and the nine executive members. "The time will be soon when you all will take over the responsibility of running the New World Order, *The Flying Doves* will be at your command to correct any situation. Planet Earth will be in your hands, should you ever need our assistance we are there to help." The Guardian said.

One of the permanent members put a suggestion. "In view of the world nations' acceptance of this fraternity which we call the

New World Order, our colleagues here feel that the name of this organisation does not sound pleasant in the present circumstances, it sound somewhat punitive. How about changing it to something more befitting to the happy *mood* this gathering of peoples it represent."

The Guardian promptly replied, "When you take charge and become the authority, do as you like. I am sure you have thought of a name."

"There are several suggestions, the one most suitable and all have agreed to is, *Fraternity of Unified Nations*, furthermore, we have also chosen a motto, '*Quo Non Ascendam*', literal translation, 'To what heights can we not ascend'.

"So be it, but after I relinquish my authority to you."

They were pleased and sworn their loyalty to Ashtok, the Supreme High.

The Guardian was happy with his achievement of completion of handing over the reins, but inwardly he was sceptical about what the world appears to be. On the surface all seemed peaceful, but deep within, to some, the change of name meant nothing. There were others who believed in what the New World Order wants to achieve, though difficult but in the long run will benefit future generations. There are also the stubborn hard liners who want to stay without any change, in principal it goes against their cultural ethics, but had to comply, fearing reprisals. Within them, existed some discontented hardliner leaders surreptitiously active to dislodge the fragile peace. In so many years they were active in sending undercover operatives to neighbouring countries to disrupt peace. In one Far Eastern nation they were exposed, which led to fiery diplomatic dialogues, their embassies were targeted by hooligans, leading to escalating border clashes.

The Guardian's request to *The Flying Doves* to mediate and help settle the issue peacefully met with failure. A third country sympathetically intervened militarily and that triggered more countries to take sides and the area turned into a fierce war zone.

The peaceful years on Earth were shattered by the Asian countries involved and to add fuel to the fire, one of them unilaterally used a nuclear device. In response there was a similar retaliation, several bombs were detonated in a short time. The situation was very grave, out of control with no hope of mediation to bring them to their senses. The Guardian and *The Flying Doves* were planning on attacking the aggressor nations but a new situation surfaced in the Middle East, perhaps encouraged by the situation in the Far East, a television station began verbal attacks on a neighbouring country accusing it of being a puppet of the aliens. Tempers rose which led to a pre-empted attack. Countries in the region took sides. Some south Asian countries provided ground and air assistance and one of them unilaterally used a nuclear device. Most unexpectedly another retaliated with the same. The Guardian had to make a decision to attack all the warring factions, or contact the Supreme High for his advice. He chose the latter, "Cannot understand how they got those nuclear missiles. All the major powers had surrendered theirs to us. All these countries must have bought and hidden a few for such an eventuality. The Far and Middle East is going up in flames." The Guardian reported.

Ashtok thought for a while and said to him, "Give me some time, I will call you back." He called Ayond and they met. "The situation is very serious, any suggestions?"

Ayond thought for a while, "When no rational reasoning can solve it, attack both sides." They were interrupted by a call from the Guardians.

"I told you to wait for me to call you." Ashtok was not pleased.

"Sorry but had to, there is an alarming news. State of emergency has been declared in the United States. Most unexpectedly an eastern Asian nation showered California, Washington and Oregon States with a new type of missiles. On approaching their targets each release several nuclear projectiles, indiscriminately causing heavy loss of life and infrastructure. But the response was more lethal. From bases in the Pacific the adversaries were no match to cause further offensive and were wiped out completely.

"Russia was not spared, from an unknown source somewhere north of Turkey nuclear missiles showered its southern borders. The Russian High Command pin-pointed the locations of the sources and hell broke loose on them. The whole atmosphere is polluted with nuclear radiation, people are suffering all over, even in the areas which were not involved. In northern and central Africa hostilities, mostly tribal, took the opportunity to settle old feuds. The whole planet is in turmoil. Satellite pictures show pathetic scenes of suffering, soon nuclear radiation will envelope the entire planet. I can do nothing to stop this madness. What are your instructions?"

"Good you called," Ashtok said to the Guardian. "From what you have said and the scenes I am watching on my screen, I suspect a clandestine network of saboteurs on an international scale are responsible for disrupting the system. Despite our sincere efforts to bring sanity to that world, some prefer to go back to their ways. I have decided not to intervene, if I do, many innocent lives will be lost in the process, don't want to add more to their miseries. Even then we will not accomplish any satisfactory solution. Not even their gods can save them now." Ashtok mused and added, "Unless he is waiting for the right moment to strike."

The Guardian was a bit confused and said, "You mean a supernatural intervention, but…"

Before he could finish, Ashtok interjected, "Never mind what I have said, it is time we left them alone to solve their miserable squabbles. You start packing, I have sent two large ships, one for the chosen families and the other for animals, leave no traces of our presence, and do not forget the butterflies and the bees."

For Ashtok the Supreme High, that world regretfully is no more his worry. With the help of Zathenfur he concentrated on Mars building more cities and preparing for the arrival of the immigrants. The weather continued to stabilise with more applications of the dark energy source. Piping the water supply from different underground locations was laborious, but successful.

"You have given this source of energy an appropriate name, *'life giver'*, better than dark energy which sounds hostile."

"It took our ancestors a very long time to understand its enigmatic influence and reactions on living and non-living matter and succeeded in controlling it, to be applied to whatever or wherever it is needed." Zathenfur said.

"We are lucky to have met, together we shall shape the destiny of the future Martian residents."

"How ironic, our ancestors did not accept your invitation to stay on Earth when calamity had struck, and now thousands of years later we have rejoined to shape new destinies. What would have been the destiny of that world had they stayed?" Zathenfur said philosophically.

"Perhaps we would have made it different from what it is now and we would be still living there."

Meanwhile, the Guardian was having a hard time finding the selected families located in the wars torn areas. In North and South America all were found. Some of the European and Russians were not traceable. To compensate for the missing families, a random selection was made from Japan, Australia and remote Pacific islands. His African contact had selected two families, one each from Ethiopia and Kenya. The total exceeded the previous number of immigrants by thirty three. He was pleased.

His next task was the collection of animals. Horses, cows, goats, sheep, stags and deer. He found the right person who had been nursing bees most of his life.

"What about butterflies, can you help?" the Guardian asked him.

"Of course, I can get different varieties and have special cages made for their transportation, provided you take me along. You will need me."

The Guardian agreed.

All was in place, just waiting for the spaceships to arrive.

It was a cold winter morning just after dawn, when the Guardian decided to have a stroll. Dressed in long overcoat, a muffler and a hat, covering most of his face to avoid recognition. His driver parked along a curb facing the ocean. He asked him to wait.

The Guardian walked a little distance and sat on bench. A few passersby hurriedly went about their business. The respites of ocean waves coming to rest along the shore was the only sound. He was happy to be alone, lost in thoughts.

Not far from where he sat, noticed a shadowy figure leaning against a lamp post. Ignored it and continued his gaze at the ocean. He turned his head to see if that shadowy figure was still there. It was gone. Before he could turn his face away it suddenly appeared.

"That is strange, my eyes must be playing tricks or perhaps it is the weather."

The figure started to walk towards him. "Probably he is as lonely as I am and wants company," The Guardian thought.

The figure stood before him blocking his ocean view.

"Have a seat, it is a wonderful morning." The Guardian said.

The figure did not respond but flung himself on to the bench which shook it from its roots.

"You know me, I have just come from your headquarters and was told that you had gone for a walk. They gave me the location. We had met before, it was with your Supreme High Ashtok."

The Guardian recognised the voice as the king of the Jinn, "What can I do for you?"

"I am here to tell you that Earth is no longer a place to live on. Many of our people have moved to other planets and moons in the solar system, a few of us remain but intent to leave soon. Please inform your Supreme High that I and some of us wish to accept his offer to move on to Urna or Mars as he had suggested."

"The Supreme High had already instructed me to advice you that you are welcome to move whenever you wish. I too will be leaving soon."

"Before I leave you, let me tell you what we always thought about the human race." The king said. "Their emergence as an entity is a long story. As you know, we the Jinn were the first to have evolved on this planet, out of different climatic conditions that existed when Earth was in its early stages of development. To put it simply, conditions were more or less similar to as are today on Titan, Saturn's moon. However, many millions of years a new type of lifeform began to emerge, very similar to Homo sapiens and developed to be a progressive intelligent race, but they did not live in harmony, fought each other and created chaos. Nature intervened, the planet came in the grip of an ice age and there was total extinction of all life. Millions of years later there was re-emergence of the same species in the form of Homo erectus and Homo sapience. From their past knowledge the Jinn knew that humans will ultimately be like their predecessors, they will be no better. The Jinn wanted to exterminate them, but unanimous decision by their elders vetoed against it, hoping they may develop to be better. Today, we are witnessing another chapter that may lead them to their untimely demise. With these thoughts I leave you hoping to meet again in a better world." The king of the Jinn got up, put both his hands on the Guardian's shoulders and faded away.

The Guardian sat thinking about what was told to him. "It looks like this is the end of another era of life as we know it on this floating rock. Perhaps it is common in the universe for life to start and end in different forms like the people who made me and Ashtok. But in their case it was not war or a fault of their own, it was nature that did it, caused sterility in living beings and plants. That is how the universe plays its game, gives and takes away. Can't complain. That is perhaps how the ball bounces, an expression I learnt from one of our friend now happily residing on Urna." The Guardian knew that it would be the last time to enjoy the solitude to be alone on a bench he had sat on hundreds of time.

Few days later he received a message from the captains of the two spaceships due to arrive in two days. On a selected location by the Guardian both landed in their invisible form. One for the immigrants and the other for the animals.

Collecting the animals was an easy task. From the zoo his team collected all that was on the list by an order from the Guardian which no one could refuse. The bees and butterflies were brought by the apiarist who also happened to be a lepidopterist specialising in butterfly studies. They were transported to the ship. It took the whole night to complete the operation.

The Guardian thought of Noah's Ark. "I have always wondered how he had done it, with wild and docile animals gathered together from different far flung areas with hardly any help. What kind of a boat was it to hold them? An unlikely fable. Perhaps after a localised flooding of an area someone who had survived, and with good imagination in his or her old age concocted a story which he or she narrated to a younger generation."

Next were the immigrants. The location selected where all were to assemble and be picked up by the spaceship was Stanley Park in the city of Vancouver, Canada. A special arrangement was made to close the park for three days. The Guardian's security team with the collaboration of the local police secured the parameters from trespassers and prodding public. The authorities were not told about the real reason for use of the park, but were told a fabricated story about a special ritual celebration by some obscure cult.

A large tent was pitched with all the amenities for the arrival of the immigrants. Three sides of the park are surrounded by water, security concentrated on the side connected to the mainland. To avoid any unnecessary suspicions and commotion during the arrival of the immigrants, the local police were requested by the Guardian's security personnel to leave and return three days later when the ritual festivity begins. Late at night the spaceship in its invisible form landed near the sea side of the Park. Small crafts also invisible picked the immigrants from their homes in different parts of the world and transported them to the park. In two nights the operation was complete.

On the third day when the local police arrived they were astonished to see the park teaming with men, women and children frolicking all over. When they asked, how and where from they arrived, they were simply told, "they arrived late last night." Inquisitive onlookers began to gather, the Guardian's security men and the local police politely asked them to leave. It was no use, more collected and it was becoming unmanageable. More help came with several police cars with their sirens blustering. On microphone an announcement requested the bystanders to leave and not to distract those who had gathered to perform their rituals. It had no effect. The public became more curious seeing some carrying bags and children with their pets, a few with bird cages. To top it all, they began to form a queue. The situation became more puzzling and the spectators scrambled to watch. It was becoming more unruly, police siren alerted to stay orderly.

Someone shouted, "Who are those people and what are they doing carrying personal effects, queueing up as if boarding a train or an aircraft. Are they crazy?"

"They must be on drugs, imagining to go somewhere." Someone in the crowd shouted back.

"Where to?" Another asked.

"May be hallucinating a ladder and want to climb up to heaven." There was a burst of cynical laughter.

"Someone call the police." Another called.

"They are all over, can't you see their cars or are you too on drugs."

"Ask them to find out why this strange mascaraed?"

The line began to move and was getting shorter, though at first it was not noticeable. A woman onlooker bellowed, "Am I seeing things, those people are vanishing into thin air, call emergency, we have a crazy situation here." She became hysterical.

"Calm yourself, emergency is all around us, may be they are taken away somewhere to a better life, why worry." One of the Guardian's security men calmly said.

She looked at him in disgust, "You are as crazy as they are, get lost" She roared.

Someone heard them and came up, "Is he troubling you?" He asked.

"No, but he thinks those people are going to heaven."

"Leave him alone, those people are practicing some kind of a ritual, the world is full of freaks."

"No ritual or freaks, they are carrying baggage and pets." She uttered nervously shaking all over.

A priest was standing close, walked up to them, "The Lord has his ways. They must be the chosen ones."

"What rubbish are you saying, I am not a child." She was mad at him.

The priest knelt and began to pray loud.

By then all the immigrants had embarked. The hysterical woman shouted, "Look, all those freaks have vanished, why anyone can't explain this mystery?"

The priest in a low tone whispered to her, "Don't question what is ordained….." She cut him short, looked him hard in the face, "Dozens of people have just vanished and nobody wants to know why and how, and you tell me it is ordained, either you or I must be the one under the influence…"

A security man joined in, "Calm down my good lady, don't asked silly questions, all is in order."

"Thank you my good man, you sound like an angel in disguise." The priest said.

The woman looked at the two, furious and was about to speak when the whining from the invisible spaceship filled the air followed by a strong gust of wind as it rose, made the already confused and frenzied spectators look around quizzically. A policeman close to the source ran in the direction where the ship had stood and as he stepped on the ground, impulsively whizzed up into the air as high as he could with a loud horrendous scream of pain and fell back. On impact the scorched ground sent him wriggling from side to side and crawl to a cooler area. He quickly removed his shoes, people surrounded him and he was unsure what to say. Looked up and managed four words, "The ground was hot."

"Must have been hot enough to propel you like a rocket, someone said and they laughed mockingly.

One of his colleagues picked one of the shoes, examined it and said, "Look at its sole, it is scorched, almost melted."

At that moment the woman making the commotion earlier busted in, "I told you this is a crazy place, nobody listens, where is the law? They must be part of it"

A policeman standing by her side said, "Ma'am, I am the law, go home and have a strong cup of coffee.

She looked at him angrily, grunted and made a rude sign.

On the spaceship the Guardian was talking to some of the crew. "That was a big risk we took, everyone there saw people disappearing into thin air, I am sure many fictional stories will be made and no one will know the truth."

"It is all over, we now look forward to our return home." A crew said.

During the journey few families experienced nausea and an uneasy feeling in their abdomen, handled meticulously by the ship's medical team. On the other ship the animals were having a more acute problem. Some stopped eating, became sluggish and rested on their bellies. Had to be fed with liquid diet. Surprisingly, just before reaching Urna when the ship's speed decelerated, they struggled and stood on their feet.

The settlers were accommodated in a complex with round-the-clock supervision. Six months later they were introduced to wearing space suits and facial masks, familiarising them with living on Mars. "These must be worn only when you step out of the domed city, inside the air is normal as it is here." They were told.

Ashtok and the Guardian shared the same accommodation. They kept a constant watch on Earth. The broadcasts said the same over and over again about the wars and the sufferings. Ashtok came out with a remark that puzzled his companion. "I can't explain it, but recently while witnessing those scenes something within me is causing a kind of a *feeling* never acknowledged before, as if my receptors are in conflict in understanding how to judge present occurrences unfolding before my eyes. Though you and I were programmed to inflict harm to wrong doers but watching it being administered lethally on one another by persons of the same species is surely a struggle for us to grasp the situation. We have witnessed wars before, but not to this scale which is likely to cause total annihilation created by the same species."

"Not in my case," The Guardian said, "I view it differently, people are always in conflict with each other, whether for territorial gains, political or religious beliefs. My job is to maintain order, not to judge who is right or wrong, I follow command to administer it. I was made by you and our people made you as a super machine. They may have implanted in you components of wisdom which kept on generating itself; enhancing your knowledge and abilities indefinitely. Perhaps right now you are experiencing a stage of change. The dreadful events on Earth must have impulsively activated a section in your receptors to grasp the moral point of view of condition never experienced before."

"Your analysis may be right, my makers did plant in me a self-generating catalyst that gives me the ability to improve on my understanding like a normal brain keeps progressing to learn as time moves on. I am impressed with your observation, being called the Guardian is appropriate in view of all your faculties. To change the subject, I am happy with the new arrivals. It will be soon when we will move them to Mars. Ayond and her colleagues visit them regularly, tuning them for the Martian conditions." Ashtok concluded.

Several weeks had passed. More domed cities were completed. A selection of twenty families was made based on their fitness, the rest needed more time to adjust. Accompanied by Ashtok, the Guardian, Ayond and her colleagues, medics, nurses and attendants, were flown to their new home. The children dashed aimlessly shrieking with joy. Parents tried to stop their surges, Ashtok asked them not to, "Let them be, soon they will have their fill and calm down. The attendants will take you to your allocated quarters. There do as you like, but don't attempt on going outside. The main door to the city is closed electronically,

240

only staff members are authorized to operate it. Once you settle down, a staff member will continue the training of wearing the outdoor suits and masks. Soon others will join you and stay in the adjoining complexes which are all connected with tunnels for your easy excess to meet each other. Before I leave, I want to welcome you for being the first human immigrants, you are now Martians. Enjoy it, we will be back soon to check on you."

Ashtok and his entourage left and boarded *The Gentle Stream*. A voice from within the ship exclaimed, "Hello all"

Ashtok and the Guardian recognised the towering figure of the king of the Jinn. "What are you doing here?"

"Ashtok I have come to congratulate you for bringing the very seditious race that has brought about destruction and misery to our beloved earth. Now you are planting those very seeds on this virgin soil."

"I know what I am doing, these are well selected people, give them a chance to prove themselves."

"Your very words ring a bell, some of our ancestors echoed the same words millions of years ago and the rest humbly submitted. They was wrong."

The king walked up to Ayond, "You look as young and beautiful as ever, how about visiting our new abode sometime?"

"Where is it now?" Ashtok asked.

"Jupiter's moon Ganymede, we had planned our move some time ago, it has many features suitable for us. Remember those creature you encountered on Europa, who look like Kangaroos, we had moved them from there."

"That was a cruel thing to do."

"But they are happy now, you have provided them with companions from Mars and enriched their food resources."

"How did you find out?"

"We are Jinn, keep our eyes open to what goes on everywhere and thanks to Ayond for eradicating those reptilian creatures from Io some years ago. Let me tell you before I forget, when your planet Urna became a member of the solar system and you deserted it, our people helped the survivors to reconstruct what was left of their world."

"So it was your race that performed the noble gesture. We were told some unknown race came to their recue, which we dismissed since no living beings other than humans were known to exist. And for your information, we did not abandon them, we had no idea of their predicament until much later."

"Well that was in the past. Coming to the present, you have promised to house some of us on Urna, and what about a city of our own on Mars. You have called the first three, *Ayond, Lincoln and Galileo*. I have to think of a suitable name for ours, perhaps *Earth,* to remind us of our birth place.

"You come over to Urna and chose a location suitable for your people. Same will apply to you on Mars. You can come along with us if you wish."

"Thank you Ashtok, I am with some of our people, will meet you soon."

All the immigrants were accommodated in five domed cities. The Marants domed cities were built above their underground habitat where they could freely move in and out as they pleased. The *Ayond* city was kept for Ashtok and his colleagues. The king of the Jinn chose to build their city further north.

The weather on Mars was unpredictable, sometimes heavy showers but mostly dry spells. On many parts moss like foliage has shown promising signs and in due course shrubs and plants will take root. The planet on the whole is vitalising satisfactory.

"I remember the time when you asked me to visit Mars and look into the possibility of reviving it just in case something happens to Urna and we have to move over there. Well, we have succeeded, and Urna is still there and I prefer living on it." The Guardian said to Ashtok as they sat watching television.

"The crazy war on Earth is still going on, millions must have perished and the nuclear contamination must have spread causing havoc. What a waste, at this rate it will put them back hundreds of years."

"It is no more our problem, we will just watch and see their untimely demise." Ashtok said and added, "The king of the Jinn is back on Urna, I wish to invite all, how about next week."

Invitations were sent to the king of the Jinn, Zathenfur, Ayond and their colleagues and few seniors from Urna. He asked David to select some music discs from the library.

Ayond arrived early and Ashtok requested, "I know nothing about hosting and can you please do it for me."

The guests arrived and the party began with soft music in the background. Ayond drew everyone attention, "Like old times we are all together, as happy as can be, all due to Ashtok our Supreme High and his assistant the Guardian. By their wisdom and care we have survived many ordeals going back from the moment our world Urna was jettisoned out of its parental home thousands of years ago right up to this moment. All of us are happily settled and because of them earned many new friends and opened doors to new homes in this solar system. I request our host to say a few words."

Ashtok began, "Ayond you too must be credited for what we had achieved, though you came much later. The Guardian and I are made differently, will continue to go on with an occasional change of a nut or a bolt to put it simply. The ordeal our planet endured during our journey into the unknown when it was shunted out of its parental solar system, would have continued sailing indefinitely until all life ceased to exist and we two remained as its only occupants, continue drifting indefinitely, crash onto another sphere or perhaps plunge into a sun. Instead we cruised comfortably into this solar system and got a new home. We cannot forget our stay on Earth, there we earned the company of many friends including you the king of the Jinn. Sadly we had to leave it. Mars has awakened, when in full blooms it will compete with its neighbour. I would also like to thank Zathenfur and his people, their ancestors shared living on Earth for a long time as we did; in fact earlier from the time humans were entering the age of being the first civilization. We all became part of that heritage and loosely claimed to be earthlings and we miss it. I shan't keep you much longer, let the party begin with zest and laughter." Ashtok then turned to the king of Jinn, "By the way you never told us your name."

The king walked to Ashtok, "Beautifully spoken and by the way I have no name, being a king, don't need one."

Music filtered softly and the guests formed groups and chatted. On occasions loud laughter punctuated the ambiance, drowning the music.

The king of the Jinn came up to Aishtra, "Curious to know how you got to be with the aliens. Don't you ever feel like returning to your people?"

"I was a child when I was rescued and brought up by Ayond, she became a mother to me. Now happily married to Sam, a human, I am very much at home here."

Saeed the Egyptian narrated why he left Egypt, "After I gave Ayond the device found in the pyramid, months later the museum authorities discovered that it was missing. There was a long investigations, suspicion fell on me. I had to escape, went to London."

"That was the right decision, by the way there is a rumour going around in the museum, you plan to marry an Urna girl, one of your assistance." Jim said.

"Yes Jim, and thank you all, I am indebted to your team, good thing I met you all in Egypt. I would have been still escorting tourist and telling them how great we were."

"Why have you not brought your fiancé to the party?"

"She is here, talking to Zathenfur, do you want to meet her?"

They walked up to Zathenfur. Saeed introduced the charming girl to Jim. "I am impressed by the knowledge this beautiful lady has on the mythical legend of Atlantis as described by Plato and some others. Do you mind if she can work with us?" Zathenfur asked.

"I cannot spare her, she is fully attached to our museum and library, besides soon we are getting married."

They were joined by Sam, Daniel and Fiona. "Tell me Zathenfur, have you found the girl of your dreams. I am sure there are some in your community." Fiona said.

"Yes and no, none that would replace the one I lost, who looked like you."

"I know how you feel, but you have a long life ahead, begin to face reality."

"You may be right, I will keep my eyes open and you will be the first to know."

"How about refreshing our drinks before dinner is served." Sam suggested.

After dinner they relaxed on the open terrace. Ashtok walked about with the Guardian, "How happy I am to be with these wonderful people. There is nothing more I can ask for." Ashtok said.

They were interrupted by an attendant. He handed Ashtok a piece of paper.

On reading it, he asked, "Where is the person who gave you this?"

"Waiting outside."

He walked out and returned. "Ladies and gentlemen, sorry to interrupt, we have an alarming news, please follow me to my study."

Ayond was conversing with David, "Now what is so important that we go there?"

"Perhaps to see more of those horrendous war scenes." David said calmly.

"What can be more alarming from what is going on Earth?" She said.

They entered his spacious study with chairs and sofas. Some remained standing. On the wall there were three screens side by side. "There is some alarming news coming from Earth." Ashtok announced.

"Perhaps the wars have escalated and more countries are roped into it." Ayond added.

Ashtok began, "I have been alerted by our earth moon-base that a phenomena of some kind, a dense deliquescent wave is sweeping across Japan, stealthily devouring all it touches, life and infrastructure, moving steadily westwards."

All three screen were on, transmitting from satellites, one showing war scenes and another planet Earth from space, both muted and the third a Japanese crew in a vehicle filming the mysterious advancing wave. The vehicle moved progressively capturing horrific scenes. The wave rose to about fifty feet high bulldozing and melting whatever was in its path. Anything higher than that was not affected. The crew came to a stream and were trapped, their only option was to jump into the water and swim. But they were not fast enough and met an agonizing death as the surge caught up with them.

They watched in horror as the wave of death crossed over to China. "Soon it will devour the whole of Asia, Europe and Africa will be next. The Americas will not escape. The entire planet will be scraped from its roots. It is a horrible way to go." Ashtok said.

"Excuse me Ashtok, this can't be possible, some Hollywood special effect artists must have created these images to put fear and deescalate the wars. Not likely that natural phenomena could do this." David said.

"I don't think so, Let me unmute the second screen showing the planet and zoom in on Japan and China." It showed both landmasses being swept clean of any trace of human existence. "Amazingly, the sea in between was unaffected. The surge or whatever it is had no effect on water or anything higher than fifty feet. There is some hope for those living on higher grounds or mountains. Sill cannot figure out what could have caused it. I wonder if those nuclear devices exploding all over Asia, the Middle East, Europe and North America had triggered some cosmic element to cause its birth. It might run out of fuel and stop." Ashtok surmised

He switched back to the screen showing the news. '.... We are experiencing a phenomena since an hour ago.' The broadcast said.

"Experiencing what?" Someone asked.

"Please listen, do not interrupt," Ayond said softly.

'…..scientists can't figure it out. Satellite images of the sun are showing normal flow of light, what is causing this glitch is beyond explanation. Our cameras are pointing to the sky. Just watch.' A brilliant sunshine and blue sky suddenly went dark, no sunlight, then came back and went off again. The scenes continued for some time. The announcer added, "It is like being in a room with someone playing with the light switch."'

Ashtok said, "There is only one logical conclusion, whatever gave birth to that messy substance must be responsible for the atmospheric discrepancy. You can see on the second screen the sun is shining normally."

Zathenfur was listening attentively, looked at Ashtok, "You may be right. We are witnessing the demise of a unique world. Billions of years in the making, building and rebuilding, shaping the topography for the emergence of life, had its ups and downs and now regressing rapidly to be as barren as Mars was."

"Correction Zathenfur, not as barren, Mars had no water on its surface, but Earth has all its water intact, besides all humanity will not perish, those living on mountains will survive, but the cultivated lands will surely be scraped clean, same for the industrialised world. Survivors will have to start from the very beginning."

"One of you is a pessimist and the other an optimist," the king of the Jinn interjected. "I am neither. But I can confidently say, whatever world will emerge from this catastrophe will not be any better than what it was before. We were lucky to have moved out from there well in time."

Zathenfur thoughtfully said, "Had we not accepted Ashtok's advice to settle on Urna and had gone there, we would have met the same fate. I was just talking to one of our scientist who is here with us, and he said to me, from our records while we were harnessing the power of the dark energy on a barren planet in the Orion constellation, a similar phenomenon had occurred. The radiation level increased many folds, and a strange element emerged, a singularity of some sort, just like the one we are witnessing. The amplified shower of nuclear bombardments must have triggered the elements. Do you have any ideas, Ashtok?"

"From what you have theorised, I am beginning to see a possibility. It is perhaps ...." He paused. "No, too farfetched. I will ponder over it."

Hours passed and all were deeply engrossed watching scenes of annihilation of life and infrastructure.

"You are free to stay here as long as you like, I would prefer we witness the final closing chapter." Ashtok suggested.

David philosophically said in a low voice, "Days ago on either side of a vibrating with life Earth, were the lifeless planets, Mercury and Venus and on the other side Mars, the new order emerging will be three dead planets in a row with the fourth just about to blossom.

Ayond retorted from somewhere behind, "What about Urna? Don't we exist somewhere in that order?"

"My gracious lady, I am referring to the original planets the solar system was made of, before Urna's arrival. Our sun gave birth to this family, it was she, meaning the sun which much later saw a helpless child drifting aimlessly in space, extended its loving hand and gave it a home, adding to the grandeur of this wonderful household."

"Well put David." Sam interjected, "Urna's presence has changed the sequence of events, not only ours but also of those with us who had contributed to bringing life to a sleeping world, meaning Mars. Mankind shall live on. Destiny had sent a helping hand from afar, the chain of events started when Urna began its journey out of its binary system millenniums ago. Furthermore I can add, that journey of theirs was *meant to be* for the continuation of our species that would have been erased from existence."

"Sam I like what you have just said, those were words of wisdom, beautifully annualized." Ayond said.

"While you are reminiscing, let me add another," the king of the Jinn butted in. "Our species is the oldest inhabitants in the solar system, we evolved much before the single-cell amoeba. Our kind have seen it all. You will be astonished with what I am about to tell you.

"In the beginning, Mars was the only world in the solar system bubbling with life, Earth was just in the process of shaping itself, preparing for the emergence of life. Our evolution began much earlier when the planet was in its infancy, to put in a simple way, it was similar in conditions as on Saturn's moon Titan. We evolved out of those environments, hence our exclusive physical traits. Electromagnetic forces gave a helping hand. Much later, just a few million years ago hominins evolved.

Between Mars and Jupiter was another planet, a little bigger than Earth's moon, inhabited by the Martians. A stray planetoid crashed into it causing what is today the asteroid belt. Mars was showered with meteorites and horrendous bolts of electric surges. A few Martians managed to escape, went to Earth. Humans at that time were just developing into a species. The Martians settled on a continent in the middle of the Pacific Ocean. Being in the zone of the ring of fire, a volcanic and earthquake prone area. Years later it broke into bits and pieces and sank, leaving behind the Polynesian islands that dot the Pacific Ocean. Some moved to Asia and Europe. Interbred with hominins and resulted in a host of different species, one of them was the Homo sapiens who inherited their genetic characteristics. The Neanderthals were an offshoot. The irony of it is, all humans have some of the Martian DNA in them. The immigrants brought by you have it, transported back to their original home, thanks to Ashtok."

"Very interesting, you seem to have volumes of information as we have about our own former solar system and some of the constellations visited by us, not to mention our odyssey to Alpha Centauri." Zathenfur said.

"How about you Ashtok, tell your story about the world you were made on, and your subsequent move to Urna, some of our new residents may be interested to know." Ayond requested Ashtok.

Ashtok wanting the festivity to move on rather than narrate tales of the past, said softly, "It is a long story, we'll leave it for another occasion. But I can tell you, the world I was made on was run by a wonderful race, their aim in life was to improve their environment, they outlawed wars and concentrated on technological development. Right now how about going back to the lounge and put on some loud music and let the floor vibrate under your feet."

Jim, at the back of the room got up from his chair, "Before that I have a few words. Back on Earth I collected antique books and artifacts, studied old languages and the like, but had never heard such fascinating tell tales as have transpired in here. I am reminded and I will quote from Shakespeare's Hamlet,

'And therefore as a stranger give it welcome,

There are more things in heaven and earth, Horatio,

Than are dreamt of in your philosophy.'"

Jim's wife uttered, "Why don't you ever quote such meaningful words when at home."

"Because you never let me, *you* talk all the time!" Jim blurted.

Laughter filled the room.

Daniel raised a hand, "May I have your attention please." He said with a dramatic gesture. "With your permission Ashtok, I also have something to say."

"Yes Daniel, love to hear what your thoughts. In your early life down there on Earth you were a priest, a man of God, what do you think has happened?"

Daniel began, "I am still a man of God but not as we viewed Him there. Here on Urna after learning from your great sages have understood the philosophy of a deity that should exists only within, and not outwardly, meaning, to display His existence by decorative images and artifacts to satisfy the natural instinct to have something to feel and touch. That is archaic. He is patient and watching, like you Ashtok, you watched and guided the best you could, when you failed, left them to face their predicament, could have gone the other way to reprimand by your powers, but you did not. You and I are the same though made differently, but within have an element of compassion, you left them alone. But in my analysis He knows best when to strike like in Noah's floods or the hell fire on Sodom and Gomorrah. Those were localised events punishing communities. This time it is not a community but the whole world, their atrocities have gone far, they must be stopped. Just swept the carpet from under their feet. He knew their so called love for Him is hypocritical.

"Finally I have to say, remembering the Book of Daniel and about his interpretation of Nebuchadnezzar's dream and his own in which he said, 'The dragon stood on the shore of the sea. And I saw a beast coming out of the sea.' As far as I am concerned what is happening on Earth; the beast is the lethal wave which is devouring what it touched."

"Thank you Daniel, stimulating indeed." Ashtok politely acknowledged. "Listening to what has been said here, Zathenfur has enlightened us with what had happened on a planet while harnessing the dark energy and Daniel has explained the phenomena from a theological point of view. Both have credence and made it easy for me to make a guess and analyse the situation happening on Earth, scientifically. I would say an anomaly was created due to the nuclear bombardments, the radiation triggered and unleashed the fibers and filaments to interact in an element to infuse, and activate the latent deadly features in an invisible substance called dark matter."

No one spoke after that deliberation. They were digesting what was said. To change the ambiance, Ayond broke the silence, "I think we all move to the lounge and have some refreshments and continue with your chats there."

A few hours later they returned to the study to witness the cataclysmic trails left behind by the mysterious invisible terminal force leaving behind a lifeless barren brown landscape.

CHAPTER 26

The Earth flag left behind by the four astronauts who were ceremoniously booted out from Mars was placed in the Urna museum. Beside it a screen displayed scenes from Earth, of metropolitan cities with busy streets, farms and cattle grazing, landscapes and rivers with boats, clips from Hollywood comedy shows, the Statue of Liberty, Big Ben, the Eiffel Tower, the great wall of China and the show went on throughout the day. Visitors could spent hours watching.

Earth continued to be seen through satellite transmissions which were regularly maintained by bases on the moon. Showing desolate and barren landscapes, but the oceans remained active and alive. Waves continued to lash against cliffs or break gently on shorelines. Phenomenally, the giant mountain ranges, with their slopes and peaks covered with snow were intact. A scene showed a large chunk of ice breaking off Greenland's southern tip crashing, causing gigantic waves. Another pleasant sight was the flight of birds cruising in formation heading to some unknown destination.

Ayond sitting with her colleagues and Zathenfur chatted informally, David said in a comic tone, "The basic ingredients for life are intact, I wonder if Ashtok is considering revitalising."

"And perhaps move some of us down there." Jim added jokingly.

"Go to a dead world, it will be a long time before anyone would want to go there, we will be dead and gone." Sam said.

"I think Jim is referring to some of the younger migrants." Ayond explained.

"That won't be soon, perhaps in the far future. To continue bouncing from one planet to the other, come to think of it, is an interesting thought. I Remember the king of the Jinn did mention that sometime ago the Martians went there, so what we are saying now is to carry on the cycle of hopping to and fro indefinitely." David said sardonically.

"Why don't we change the subject and think about next month's Argoshtak event, the once in three years phenomena when Urna is blessed with splendour and joy. I am hosting with food and refreshments never tasted before by any of you." Ayond said warmly, then added, "You too Ashtok, I will have a specially made tea served in a specially made device for your adenoidal receptors, not only will it give you the pleasure of *sniffing* the fragrance but also to covey the *taste*. Being a machine, you too will enjoy the ecstasy of this beverage."

On Earth, somewhere in the Carpathian Mountains of Romania, below the naturally engraved head which looks like sphinx, inside a cave a sound disturbed a resting butterfly, it fluttered aimlessly within and headed toward the sunny orifice. What caused it to dislodge itself was the dragging of feet against the gravelled floor of the cave. Drowsy and disoriented a young man and a woman holding to each other for support sauntered out.

"We must have stayed long, we hid in a perfect place no one could find us, though they came up looked around and left. No one suspected the little vent in which we hid. I know the ins and outs of this cave since I was child. When out grazing the sheep, I used to sneak up to the mountain and explore." The man said.

"We would have been lynched had they found us."

"Not you being a rich man's daughter, I would have surely gone to prison or killed."

"Pity that my parents rejected you for being the son of a shepherd. We are safe now, no one is around, we can go to another town or village and forget the past."

They sat on a rock outside the cave and devoured what was left of their rations. The young man's eyes caught the oddness of the landscape. "To me everything looks different. What has happened to the trees and the green grass down in the valley? The stream is there, no sheep or any other animal." He said curiously and got up. The butterfly returned hovered above them and flew away.

They had no idea of the trauma the world had gone through, their miraculous escape being hidden in a vent high up on the mountain had saved their lives from the catastrophic deluge. As long as they were alive they would find a way to survive. Perhaps there were many like them throughout the world who had survived by being at the right place at the right time.

The End

APPENDIX

Referred to in 'The Medallion' a novel by the same author:
(i)(iii) (vi) (viii) (xiv) (xvi)
Referred to in 'The Rescue' a novel by the same author:
(ii)(iv) (v) (vii) (ix) (x) (xi) (xii) (xiii) (xiv) (xv) (xvi)

Books by the same author

The Fatal Flaw (1987, published by Arthur H. Stockwell Ltd. Devon, Great Britain.

Journey to Life (2015, published by Wesbrook Bay Books, Vancouver, Canada.

The Medallion – (2017, published by AuthorHouse, Bloomington, IN, USA.

The Rescue – (2017, published by AuthorHouse, Bloomington, IN, USA.

Special thanks to:

Rasheda Kabir

I appreciate your proof reading help and selection of the book cover design.